the right words, when Ettie ...

she makes a birthday wish to be reunited with her missing mum, a wild magic is stirred from the sea...

## Also by Amber Lee Dodd

We Are Giants

# Lightning Chase Me Home

## Amber Lee Dodd

**SCHOLASTIC**

Scholastic Children's Books
An imprint of Scholastic Ltd
Euston House, 24 Eversholt Street, London, NW1 1DB, UK
Registered office: Westfield Road, Southam, Warwickshire, CV47 0RA
SCHOLASTIC and associated logos are trademarks and/or
registered trademarks of Scholastic Inc.

First published in the UK by Scholastic Ltd, 2019

Text copyright © Amber Lee Dodd, 2019

The right of Amber Lee Dodd to be identified
as the author of this work has been asserted.

ISBN 978 1407 19165 2

A CIP catalogue record for this book
is available from the British Library.

Printed by CPI Group (UK) Ltd, Croydon, CR0 4YY
Papers used by Scholastic Children's Books are made
from wood grown in sustainable forests.

1 3 5 7 9 10 8 6 4 2

This is a work of fiction. Names, characters, places, incidents
and dialogues are products of the author's imagination or are used
fictitiously. Any resemblance to actual people, living or dead,
events or locales is entirely coincidental.

www.scholastic.co.uk

*For my parents, who taught me to read.*

*And for you, dear reader, whose adventures are only just beginning.*

*Chapter 1*

Early on the morning of my eleventh birthday I was standing in the harbour wearing mismatched shoes and holding a lobster. This is not how birthdays should start. If Mum was still here, we would be in our pyjamas eating pancakes. Or if I lived anywhere else in the world but Dark Muir Island, I would still be in bed sound asleep at six in the morning. Instead, I was standing under a starry sky, unpacking Da's fishing boat.

"But why do we have to go out on the boat?" I asked Da as we clambered aboard. It smelled of lobster pots that had been left out in the sun too long. This is not something you ever want to smell, especially first thing in the morning.

"Because it's tradition, Amelia. Every islander has to go and touch the rock when they turn eleven. I did it, your grandpa did it, your great grandpa did it," Da said, passing me our dog Pipi.

"Did Mum do it?" I interrupted.

"No, she wasn't an islander," Da said quietly. "This is something special, just for us folk." He still didn't like me talking about Mum, even if it had been nearly two years since she left.

Da started the engine and turned the wheel with his big weather-worn hands.

But it didn't feel very special. In fact, it felt terrifying. For a start, I hated being out on the choppy waves because I always got seasick. And secondly, I was a bit scared of where we were going.

Just off the harbour of Dark Muir Island is a glistening black rock called the Serpent's Tooth. It's said that a great snake stirred the seas and made all the Scottish islands rise up here. But when the snake had finished it was so tired that it laid down on the sea floor and died. Now all that's left of it is one giant black tooth, which pokes out of the sea even in the highest tides. Whenever any islander turns eleven they're meant to swim out and touch it. But I'm a rubbish swimmer and only half an islander, as all the other kids like to remind me. I don't even look like an islander. I'm not pale and redheaded like my da. I look exactly like my mum: dark, curly-haired and freckled all over. The only thing about me that's different to her is my eyes. I have my da's eyes. Not blue, or brown or green, but some colour in the middle, and changeable with the weather. On a clear, cold summer's day they look blue, and out on the boat in the early morning light they look green. But most of the time they look grey. The kind of grey the sky turns just before a big storm.

My eyes were grey that day. Even though it was the middle of August, even though the sea was calm and I could hear Da whistling over the thrum of the engine, I could feel something in the air. On Dark Muir Island there is always a storm just over the horizon. There are autumn storms when the wind is so strong that the trees grow bent the following year. And the winter storms, when the boats in the harbour shudder and shake and threaten to break free from their moorings. Then there are spring storms when the thunder and lightning chase you home. And finally there are even summer storms, when the rain is hot and hard. The closer we got to the rock the more I could feel something brewing. And it wasn't like any storm I had felt before.

"We're here, hen," Da said as he cut the engine. The boat rocked back and forth unsteadily on the choppy sea.

3

*Ar row row*, Pipi barked at the waves as if she could get them to still. In her head Pipi believes she's a great big dog even though she's a funny sort of tiny mixed-up terrier, with ears too big for her head and legs too short for her body. Pipi finally fell quiet as the boat settled under the huge shadow of Serpent's Tooth Rock. Da looked at me expectantly like I was meant to know what to do next.

"Well, go on and touch it then," he said.

I looked down at the water. It was so dark I couldn't see my own reflection. Grandpa had told me the deepest part of the ocean is over seven miles away. And down there it's so dark that the fish don't need eyes. Just thinking about it made me shiver.

"You just have to lean over and touch it. You don't have to go in the water," Da told me.

I shook my head.

"All the other bairns have done it. Don't you want to be like your friends?" Da said, pulling at his big red beard.

I couldn't tell Da that being the weird home-schooled kid made it impossible to make friends. But I didn't want to let him down. So I took a deep breath, tried not to think about fish with no eyes, and leant over the side. My fingertips wouldn't quite reach, however far I stretched. Pipi kept barking and spinning around in little circles. She wasn't the only one who knew this wasn't a good idea.

"I've got you," Da said, grabbing me by the waist and hoisting me forward until my feet were in the air and I was dangling over the sea. I squeezed my eyes shut, stretched out my arm and laid the palm of my hand flat on the stone. It wasn't cold like I was expecting; it was warm, like it was alive.

"Make a wish," Da said.

But I didn't know what to ask for. I knew what Da wished: that I would do well at my new school. Mum had home-schooled me since I was seven, after my teacher Mrs Stokes labelled me "unteachable". Then when Mum left, Da and Grandpa had tried to continue the lessons, but they were too impatient (Da) and distracted (Grandpa) and I learned about as little as I had with Mrs Stokes. So Da had signed me up for Bridlebaine Academy, the fancy school on the neighbouring island that he went to when he was a kid, and hadn't stopped talking about all summer: about how much I would learn, and all the clubs I could join, and how many new friends I would make. I wanted to believe everything Da was saying: that I'd get to join the drama class and be popular with everyone. But as much as I was looking forward to starting school, a part of me ached for things to go back to the way they'd been before, with me taking lessons with Mum. But she was gone and it had now been nearly a year since she last called on the phone to speak to me. The worst part was I didn't even know where in the world she was. So I had to use my imagination. Sometimes I pictured Mum charting her way through the Amazon, or riding camels through the desert. Sometimes I even imagined her in not so nice places like the freezing North Pole, so I wouldn't wish I was with her so much. But birthdays were hard. I would have given all of my presents just to be with Mum, even if it meant living on an iceberg in the middle of the Antarctic.

"Come on, Amelia, hurry up and make a wish," Da said, his arms beginning to shake.

I leaned forward and touched the rock again.

"I wish I could be with Mum," I whispered, and it could have just been my imagination but I swear I felt the rock move.

Da pulled me back on to the deck of the boat and slapped my shoulders.

"Your nana would have been so proud," he said, his eyes shining. "Now you're a real islander, Amelia, and not just part of my family, but of this whole island. Which is something very special, because it means you will never be alone now." Da hugged me and pulled me into his very best soft flannel shirt. I realized that he was making a big effort to make my birthday special and I felt a pang of guilt about my wish.

Then Da pulled two badly wrapped packages from his bag.

"I hope you like them," he said nervously.

I tore through the bubble wrap and gaffer tape he had used to cover both my birthday presents. Inside the first one was the most hideous pair of shoes I had ever seen: pink with daisy buckles. I slipped them on just to make Da happy. I knew later I would be burying them deep in the garden, where even Pipi couldn't find them. But the next present was much better. It was a huge hardback book about explorers.

"I popped into Mr Sinclair's bookshop and saw this. I thought we could replace that old tatty one with something a bit more grown up."

Da meant the picture book of women adventurers I kept under my pillow. But even though this new birthday book was beautiful and full of real photos of famous explorers, I knew it couldn't replace my one at home. It's not like it was anything special. It was just a little yellow picture book. And it was pretty old, so the spine was crumbling apart, the pages were all dog-eared and it still smelled like the banana milkshake that I'd spilled on it once. But I could never get rid of it because it was mine and Mum's book, filled with the stories she had told me when I was little, about brave and wonderful women adventuring down the Amazon and escaping from cannibals.

Mum was sort of an adventurer too. Before she moved to Dark Muir she travelled around the world filming wildlife. Once she even worked for David Attenborough on one of his documentaries. She always said how much she loved doing it, how she loved filming and sleeping under the trees in tropical rainforests. Which is why, when I closed my eyes and thought of Mum, I always saw her on some grand adventure, just like the women in my book.

"There's one more present. And this one's special," Da said. He smiled and produced another parcel from his pocket: a little red box wrapped in ribbon. He passed it to me, and it felt heavy in my hands.

"On your eleventh birthday it's tradition to pass on a family heirloom," Da said, turning around and starting the boat back up.

Inside the box was the small gold compass Nana had given to Mum on the day I was born. I gasped. Where had Da got this from? Had Mum left it behind? I looked up at Da, expecting him to explain. But his face was doing that weird expression it does when he's tired, or hungry, or in a bad mood. So I bit my lip and stared down at the compass. I watched the needle point the way back home. To the house that lay just under the big, bright North Star.

By the time we moored the boat and made our way up the steep cliff steps, it was just getting light. Light enough for me to see Grandpa through the kitchen window, pottering about slowly. When we got in we saw that he'd taken all the knives and forks out of the drawers.

"Everything's in the wrong place again," Grandpa muttered as he started moving all the pans around.

"Now, now, Da, none of your silliness today," my da replied, pulling a chair out and sitting Grandpa down.

Sometimes Grandpa forgets things. Like which drawer the forks are or that Nana's dead. Sometimes we try to remind him, sometimes we don't, but most of the time we end up putting the kitchen back together. After we had tidied up, Da went to the fridge and pulled out the biggest, messiest cake I had ever seen. It was about two feet tall, had purple and green icing, and leaned to one side.

"I made it myself," Da said proudly.

"Well it's very, it's very…" I said, searching for the right word.

"That is one ugly cake," Grandpa pointed out, as if he was reading my mind.

"Tell us what you really think," Da said huffily, before putting the cake on the table and cutting up big slices, passing them out. Grandpa just stared at his.

"I took Amelia out to Serpent's Tooth Rock today to make her wish," Da continued.

Grandpa dropped his fork. It clattered loudly on to the floor as he reached across the table and wrapped his bony hands around mine.

"It chose you, didn't it?" he demanded, his eyes dark.

"What do you mean?" I said, remembering with a shiver how I thought I had felt Serpent's Tooth Rock move when I made my wish.

"Oh, Amelia, that rock's dangerous – it grants wishes at a terrible price," Grandpa said, and his hands began to shake.

"Now, Da, don't you go scaring Amelia with one of your old wives' tales," Da said, rolling his eyes.

Grandpa's face clouded over again, and he dropped my hands and went back to eating his cake as if nothing had happened.

"You enjoy your birthday cake," Da told me, but the room felt tight and tense, like the air before a summer storm.

I let Pipi lick the frosting off my fingers under the table and tried to forget about Grandpa's outburst. He was always coming up with odd things. But the hand that had touched the Serpent's Tooth felt oddly hot as I ate the rest of my birthday cake.

# chapter 2

In bed that night I got out *The Little Book of Lady Adventurers*. I flipped open the cover and read the writing on the inside of the book for the millionth time.

*To Amelia Hester McLeod. Remember your name. Anything is possible.*

My mum had named me after her two favourite explorers, Amelia Earhart and Lady Hester Stanhope. Amelia Earhart was the first female aviator to fly solo across the Atlantic Ocean. She vanished while attempting to fly across the world. Lady Hester Stanhope was known as "Queen of the desert". She travelled across the Middle East on an Arab stallion,

13

disguised as a man with a cutlass searching for treasure, before she went very mad. I think Mum thought naming me after them would mean I'd grow up to be a brave adventurer. But I'm not very brave and I've never come close to having an adventure. I've never even left the islands! And they are possibly the most boring place in the world. So boring that most maps leave them off. If you were to look for them you'd have to trace your finger up from the pointy tip of Scotland, past Shetland and the North Sea. And there, right at the top, just as the map is about to disappear, are my islands. There are three of them: Dark Muir, where I live, Sometimes Island, which is technically only an island at high tide, and Stony Isle, which is the biggest of the three. That's where my new school is.

I was trying to picture my new school. I'd only visited it once, and me and Da were running late to meet the head teacher so I didn't actually get to look round beforehand. Then I had to do a test and I felt so miserable afterwards that I just wanted to go straight home. I was pretty sure I had failed, because no matter how hard I tried, all the questions got jumbled up in my head. I've got this problem with words. They never seem to stay still. They're always jiggling about, or sliding off the page. It takes me for ever to read anything and even then I have to skip out all the words I don't recognize. Even Mum struggled to get me reading. I had to read over *The Little Book of Lady Adventurers* so many times with her, that I learned it off by heart. I still can't read it in my head though; I have to read it out loud when I'm on my own. So I pretend I'm reading it to Pipi, who is actually a great audience and barks at the exciting bits. Mum didn't seem to mind that I was slow at some things, not like Da and Grandpa. When they tried to teach me there was a lot of yelling.

*Amelia Hester McLeod, your handwriting is unreadable.*

*Amelia Hester McLeod, your reading assignment is woeful.*

*Amelia Hester McLeod, none of these maths problems are correct.*

*Amelia Hester McLeod, why have you stuck all the pages of your workbook together?*

I had got so sick of hearing my full name that I stopped paying attention and started listening to the funny ideas in my head. The ones that whisper halfway through a maths test to fill in all the answers with the same number, or to put sticky notes all over your face, or to paint everything with Tippex until you get dizzy. In the end Da couldn't stand it any more. And poor Grandpa had become more and more forgetful. Once, halfway through a maths lesson, he decided we needed to paint the living room. We painted the whole room bright yellow and brown until it looked like a bee's belly. Da was really cross with Grandpa for a whole week afterwards. So it was a bit of a relief to be starting school. I was finally going to be like all the other kids on the island. Maybe I would become massively popular and start getting invited to other people's birthday parties. Or I would discover new talents like being an expert gymnast/rope climber. And then one day soon Mum would walk back through the door, ready to teach me about all the amazing places she had been.

I buried myself under the covers with Mum's compass and wondered where in the world she could be on my birthday. Then I made a list in the new notebook Grandpa had given me.

Places where Mum could be on my birthday and reasons why she can't make it home.

- Brazil: Mum is lost in the Amazon rainforest. A search party of six strong men and five cunning dogs have been sent out to look for her.
- Tanzania: she's currently halfway up Mount Kilimanjaro. She intended to finish climbing it before my birthday, but her guide, Mwamba, broke his leg and she's had to carry him.

- Manitoba: she's having to hide up a tree from a pack of hungry black bears. A posse of Canadian Mounted Police have been sent to find her, but a blizzard is slowing them down.
- Siberia: she's in a sledge race with a Russian named Ivan. Whoever wins gets an ice palace named after them. She wrote a letter to me explaining she would be late but there are no post boxes in the wilderness of Siberia. Obviously.

Wherever she was, I knew one thing: she had missed another of my birthdays. I had turned eleven, I had touched Serpent's Tooth Rock and I was about to start school. But I still felt the same. I was still just the lonely girl who lived on an island in the middle of nowhere, who was rubbish at reading and didn't know where her mum was.

Little did I know all that was about to change.

When I went to bed that night, the sky was filled with strange green lights shining down on Serpent's Tooth Rock, making it glow. But I didn't see any of this. I had fallen fast asleep to the sounds of Grandpa pacing in his bedroom, the drip of the kitchen tap and the snoring of a terrier who had eaten too much of my ugly birthday cake.

# Chapter 3

The morning I started at my new school, I was so nervous I forgot how to tie my shoelaces. For the record, I know how to do it. It just took me a bit longer to figure it out that day. Grandpa taught me when I was nine, telling me to close my eyes.

"It's like tying fishing knots. Your hands will remember how to do it. Just shut your eyes and let them do the work."

But today even with my eyes squeezed shut I couldn't get the knot right. It kept slipping and coming undone. And I couldn't ask for Grandpa's help because I didn't want him telling Da I still couldn't tie my own laces. Not on my very first day at Bridlebaine Academy. Finally I threw my school shoes against the wall and pulled on my old yellow wellies. Then I looked at myself in the mirror. I groaned; my uniform hadn't seemed so bad in the shop, but the purple blazer and skirt looked awful on. It didn't help that Da had bought my new uniform with "growing room". My fingers only just poked out of my blazer sleeves and there was room for two of me in my jumper. But the worst bit was the skirt. It was so itchy I felt like it was going to set my legs on fire! I tried to remind myself that the great explorer Mary Henrietta Kingsley refused to wear anything on her lower half but her thick wool skirt after it had saved her life when she fell into a pit of spikes. However, I was pretty sure I would rather face poisonous spikes then have to wear the itchiest skirt in the world. Eventually I gave up fiddling with it and headed downstairs.

Da clapped his hands together when he saw me. "So good to see another McLeod in the school colours," he said, his whole body puffing up with pride.

"She looks like she's shrunk," Grandpa said.

Da gave him a hard look as I tried to tuck in my overly long jumper.

"You'll have to watch that," Grandpa said. "I used to be six foot four. Tallest man on the island. I even got talent scouted for Scotland's goalkeeper."

Me and Da both raised our eyebrows. Grandpa was barely taller than me.

"You look brilliant," Da said. "But what's with the wellies?"

I flushed as I mumbled something about not wanting to get my new school shoes dirty, before shooting out the door towards the harbour.

To get to Bridlebaine Academy you have to take a ferry to Stony Isle. It's not a very long trip, but going to Stony Isle feels like going to the other side of the world. It's massive compared to Dark Muir, so big that you'd have to drive to get from one end to the other. It's so big it has eight post offices in five separate towns. And shops that sell everything, including sparkly shoes and football kits. It even has a hotel where tourists stay. And I was pretty sure that if you lived over there, you couldn't possibly know everyone's name, like you do on Dark Muir.

I used to dream about living somewhere big like that. A place where everyone didn't know everything about me and didn't constantly ask awkward questions. I knew as soon as I started walking down to the harbour that I would get stopped ten times, by someone wanting to give me some unhelpful advice about starting school, or remark on my new uniform, or asking after Da and Grandpa. It's not like I could hope to sneak down to the ferry either. Not when I was wearing a purple school blazer with my bright yellow wellies. But as I reached the maze of stone houses at the entrance of the harbour, nobody even looked up.

Everyone I passed was staring out to sea. And everyone was whispering. Even the Selkie Swimmers, the women from church who swim absolutely starkers all year round, including in the winter. Usually they greeted me with a nod and quick "God bless". But that day they all huddled together, sinking into their jackets so their whispers grew more muffled. I hadn't seen people act this weird since after Mum left. For a whole year, every time I went into the local shop the women would look at me and whisper and tut. But it wasn't like that today. It wasn't just gossip. People seemed scared.

Down by the ferry I could see a group of kids I knew a little.

"What's going on?" I asked Chloe Baines.

Chloe and me had taken swimming lessons together when we were little. We had both managed to not drown in Miss Hardacre's torturous four-week kelpie class, and had become best friends. But the days of me and Chloe cannonballing Miss Hardacre and telling each other our secrets seemed a very long time ago.

"I didn't know you were coming back to school," Chloe said.

"These skirts feel like they're made out of wool and fire ants," I told her with a grimace.

"I know – I have to wear two pairs of tights under mine just to stop the itching." She grinned at me and I felt a sharp surge of relief. Making friends might be easy after all. "So you really don't know what's going on?"

Before Chloe could say another word, Blair Watson turned around.

"Who are you talking to, Chloe?" she said, with a swish of her shiny hair.

Blair Watson was super popular. Partly because her mum ran the hairdressers so she always had perfect hair, partly because she was really good at sports, but mostly because it was better to be Blair's friend than her enemy. All sorts of awful things happened to people Blair didn't like. Which was why all the girls copied Blair's ridiculous hairstyle: a complicated braid that swept all around her head and into a ponytail tied with a purple bow.

As soon as Blair saw me her eyes grew wide.

"Oh my god, it's Amelia McLeod! What are you doing in that uniform, Home School? Do you even know how to do your school tie?" She stepped forward and flicked at the tie I'd had to tuck into my skirt. "Or did your da dress you?" The group of girls around her sniggered.

23

"Oh, and nice wellies," Blair snorted before turning her back on me and marching on to the ferry. The other girls swiftly followed her.

Chloe lingered just a moment longer before glancing at my wellies again and hurrying to join the others. I stared down at my bright yellow feet and fiddled with my tie. How had I managed to get everything wrong before school had even started? I walked slowly on to the ferry, not making eye contact with anyone.

With a jolt the ferry set off and I could finally see what everyone was talking about. The sea had changed colour. It was no longer the bright blue it had been on my birthday; it was dark and glistened like ice and there was something wrong about the horizon. Something missing. With an awful stomach lurch, I realized what it was. Serpent's Tooth Rock was gone!

The hand that had touched the rock when I'd made my wish started to tingle. Grandpa's words flooded into my head.

"It chose you, didn't it? Oh, Amelia, that rock's dangerous – it grants wishes at a terrible price."

But that was just old Grandpa getting confused again, wasn't it? It's not like my wish came true; I was still here and very much not with Mum. But I thought of how scared everyone seemed. And how dark and troubled Grandpa's eyes had turned when he warned me. And with a shudder I remembered how the rock had moved when I touched it. Had my wish started something terrible?

I found a hiding spot behind the ferry's lifeboat and got my book of adventurers out of my bag. Since Mum left I had been carrying it around everywhere, like my good luck charm, using it to give me advice. I'd flick to an explorer and imagine what they'd do when faced with a problem. It was stupid, but it always managed to make me feel better.

I cracked open the spine and turned to the page of one of my favourites.

## Alexandra David-Neel

A Belgian-French explorer best known for disguising herself as a Tibetan peasant and trekking some of the most remote and dangerous snowy mountain passes to reach the forbidden city of Lhasa. She became a knight of the French Legion for her daring exploration of Tibet and lived to 101. She even renewed her passport on her 100th birthday, planning to travel much more in the years ahead.

There was a black-and-white picture of her dressed in her disguise of cloaks and furs. She looked very fierce under her hood and I imagined her talking to me in a stern French voice.

"It's no point being afraid of something that hasn't happened."

I soon felt calmer, and before I knew it the ferry had docked at Stony Isle. Then we were rounded up by teachers and pushed on to a school bus. Everyone grabbed seats next to their friends until it was just me alone at the front. I'd totally failed at making a good first impression by wearing my stupid yellow wellies. I hid my feet under the bus seat and tried to pretend I didn't care.

"Are you a student too? Blimey," I heard the bus driver say. And then a very tall, very gangly boy got on to the bus. He looked at the empty seat next to me and grinned.

"Hey," he said, sticking his long legs into the aisle and pushing me up against the window.

"It's a daddy long legs," a boy at the back of the bus shouted and there was a ripple of laughter.

The boy blushed and pulled his legs up to his chest.

"Sorry about this. Bet you didn't think you'd have to sit next to a giant," he said. "I'm Tom by the way."

I smiled and tried to remember what Da had said about making a good first impression. Talking seemed like a sensible first step. But I was so nervous I wasn't sure what to say. It didn't seem to matter though, because Tom didn't wait for me to reply.

"So, first day at school. It's exciting but a bit scary, isn't it? I kept packing and repacking my bag all last night. I didn't know what to take. What did you end up bringing?"

I opened my mouth to answer but Tom kept on talking.

"I brought three yoghurts. I couldn't decide which flavour I wanted. And now I think one's leaked in my bag and all my books are sticky and smell like strawberry. Which isn't a great way to start your first day."

"No," I managed to squeak in.

"Sorry! I haven't even asked your name, have I? I get nervous and I talk too much and then I forget what I was meant to be saying in the first place. Mum says it's because I have a hyperactive mind. Grandma says it's because I'm an only child and don't have someone my age to talk to at home. But then Dad says—"Tom said, stopping dead and slapping his head. "I'm doing it again, aren't I?"

"I'm Amelia," I said, grinning.

"So, you ready for your first day at school, Amelia?"

I nodded but I wasn't sure. So far nothing I had planned was working out that well.

But when we got off the bus, it was hard to be upset about anything because I was reminded that Bridlebaine Academy was an actual castle! Well, most of the very old castle bits had fallen down and the classrooms were actually in three really big old houses. But there was still a tower and a little bit of the battlements and a ruined wall in the garden. I was beginning to get excited all over again.

When we got inside, we were taken to the assembly hall, which was huge and very grand. The room was filled with purple drapes with the school crest on them and a large, wooden stage. Then Miss Rutherford the head teacher came on stage dressed all in black apart from a row of colourful bangles and several large silver rings. The whole school fell quiet, like she was a witch who had us under a spell. She started giving a welcome speech, but it wasn't nearly as interesting as looking at all the things in the hall. There was a pair of antlers sticking out of a wooden plaque, two large swords mounted high up on the wall, and the stage had a full-sized piano on it. I could imagine doing fencing and dressing up in all kinds of mad costumes to perform in plays. I spotted Tom sitting cross-legged at the back; even sitting down he was tall. But I could see he was as pleased as me. He kept drumming a leg excitedly against the floor.

After the talk was over we were taken on something called "orientation" (which is a fancy word that means bored year elevens show you about). We were shown the science labs, with Bunsen burners and test tubes filled with mysterious bubbling things. The art room, which had strange sculptures in the corner and colourful paintings pegged up across the ceiling, and then the library. This was the most exciting bit, because the library at Bridlebaine just happened to be inside a castle tower!

Miss Rutherford joined the year elevens to give us a speech about how old the castle tower was, which turned out to be *really* old. Then everyone was sent off to meet their form tutors. Well, nearly everyone.

"Could Amelia McLeod, Gregory Wilson, Ian Ross, Beth Jones and Tom Harris stay behind?" Miss Rutherford called out.

Were we in trouble? I hadn't even properly started school yet. I couldn't be in trouble already, could I?

"Oh, Blair Watson too," Miss Rutherford added and I felt my stomach flip.

Blair barged her way through our little group, scowling at me as if it was somehow my fault she hadn't been able to go off with her friends.

"Well, I'm sure you all feel like you're settling in," Miss Rutherford said, checking her watch.

"It looks like Miss Archibald's late again." She sighed and clucked her tongue.

For a teacher, she didn't seem to like being around children very much.

"As I said in assembly," she carried on, "here at Bridlebaine Academy it's very important that every child flourishes, which is why all of you will have access to special lessons."

I held my breath. Maybe it was lessons for extra special and talented people. Maybe it was acting classes, or fencing classes with real swords. Or maybe we would get to look after the class pet, which was bound to be something exciting like an eagle or a wildcat.

Miss Rutherford carried on. "So that's why you'll be joining Miss Archibald's STAR unit, which provides extra support for those we consider to have …" She paused, searching for the right words. "Additional needs."

I looked at our little group. Even Blair was chewing her lip. Tom caught my eye, but he didn't have to say anything. We both knew what she really meant. She might as well have just said it was the STAR group for the very stupid.

# Chapter 4

It turned out STAR classes stood for Spelling and Reading. That's what it said on the door to our classroom. No one knew what the T stood for. I think it was just there to give it a name that made us feel better about needing "extra help" twice a week. The only good thing was that it was held in the castle tower. There was a little room just off the library we had been shown in orientation. From the classroom window I could see the whole school, including the playing fields and ruined castle wall. I watched a group of kids run out on the field in their PE kits. I wished I was there too. I could run faster than all the boys on Dark Muir and I could hold a handstand for six minutes until I finally got dizzy. But I couldn't do spelling or reading, so I was stuck in here.

I closed my eyes and imagined I was the queen of the castle and everyone down below were my servants. I was so busy daydreaming that I didn't notice all the other kids had taken their seats. There was Tom, sitting next to the dark-haired girl called Beth Jones who chewed the end of her hair nervously. Ian and Gregory sat together. I could tell they were best friends because they were both wearing their ties as short as possible and had matching rubber-band bracelets. And right at the back, scowling, sat Blair Watson. The only empty seat was in front of her. Obviously no one else had wanted to risk sitting there because she was way too close for comfort and also not visible.

As I sat down I could feel Blair boring hot little holes into the back of my neck with her eyes. I was pretty sure she was thinking of all the ways she could murder me and hide the body. I pulled my hair over my shoulder, so she couldn't get to it, and tried my very hardest to listen to what my new teacher Miss Archibald was saying.

"Sorry I'm a little late. I swear those steps get steeper every year," Miss Archibald huffed, setting down an enormous stack of folders next to a fish bowl on her desk.

"My name is Miss Archibald and I'm head of learning support," she said, pushing her glasses back up her nose. Miss Archibald had big round tortoiseshell glasses and thin rainbow-shaped eyebrows, which made her look like a very surprised owl.

"And this is Colin," Miss Archibald said, pointing to the fish in the bowl.

I looked at the fish disappointedly. It wasn't nearly as cool as having an eagle or a wildcat as a class pet.

After Miss Archibald finished handing out books she stood at the front of the class and started writing on the whiteboard while humming. I'd never had a proper teacher before, but Miss Archibald wasn't anything like I was expecting. Judging by the expressions on everyone else's faces, she wasn't what they'd been expecting either. But even stranger was that everyone stopped talking and fidgeting. Ian and Gregory stopped yanking each other's ties. Even Blair stopped kicking the back of my chair. All eyes were on Miss Archibald.

"You might be wondering what all these lessons are for. Well, STAR time is where we can work on classwork and homework together. But since this is your very first day and there isn't any homework yet—"

There was a collective whoop.

"I want us to work on something together. So, I think we should start our very own project. See those blue exercise books I just handed out? I want you to get out your fanciest pen and write this on the cover."

Miss Archibald wrote on the whiteboard in great squeaky pen swipes.

My Year of...

"My year of what?" asked Gregory.

"Ah, well, we don't know that yet. It might be My Year of Learning How Great Miss Archibald is," she said with a smile.

Ian and Gregory snorted.

"Or, My Year of Learning to Love School."

"Fat chance," mumbled Blair.

"Or even, My Year of Not Getting into Trouble," Miss Archibald continued, gesturing at Blair. "The point is, I want you to keep a journal and then at the end of the year I want you to fill in the title."

"But what are we meant to write about?" asked Tom.

"Well, think of this as a personal journal," answered Miss Archibald. "So I want you to write about you. What you think, what you do, where you go. But for today, I think we can start by writing down a little something about ourselves, as an introduction."

The class fell very quiet. Even Ian and Gregory were getting into it; I could see them furiously scribbling. They obviously had a lot to say about themselves.

I stared down at the little blue book. I had no idea what to write. I wasn't very good at words. Words were tricky and I never knew when sentences should stop. I liked lists. Lists were simple. Lists didn't need full stops in the right place. I could feel Miss Archibald staring at me.

"Are you stuck for something to write about?" she said.

"It's more that I don't know how to write it," I admitted.

"Ah, sometimes I get stuck with that too." Miss Archibald smiled. "How about you imagine you're writing a letter. Can you think of someone you'd like to write to?"

I chewed my lip. I knew who I wanted to write a letter to more than anyone else in the world. Mum. But Mum was probably somewhere far away avoiding icebergs in the arctic or discovering secret cities in the Tibetan mountains like Alexandra David-Neel. She was most definitely somewhere it was impossible to send letters to or from, otherwise I'd have heard from her. But I couldn't tell Miss Archibald that. So I just nodded my head.

"Just think about what you would like to tell them and start there," Miss Archibald said. "You give that a try and if you get stuck, just give me a shout." She winked.

I opened my blue exercise book.

Dear Mum,

It's been 711 days since you left.

I wrote. Then I thought really hard about all the things I wanted to tell her. But there were too many. So I scribbled out the Dear Mum bit and started again.

Things you've missed since you left.

- I turned eleven, touched Serpent's Tooth Rock and made a wish
- I've started a new school and have to sit in front of the most terrifying girl on the island
- Grandpa is convinced strange and terrible things are about to happen to me

PS. We got a dog. Her name's Pipi and yesterday she ate all the cheese in the house and half her wicker basket. I think you would like her.

I had dug my pen so hard into the paper that the last bit went all blobby and smudgy and when I looked up Tom was staring at me.

"What?" I hissed, quickly covering up my horrible wobbly writing.

"Nothing," he said, darting his eyes back down to his notebook.

I went back to dabbing at my page.

"It's just I have a rubber that rubs out biro."

"Really?"

"Oh yeah, I didn't know what I'd need for the first day and Grandma said I should be prepared, so I packed a bit of everything," Tom said before he pulled out the biggest pencil case known to mankind.

He rummaged around, producing a rainbow of gel pens, markers, highlighters, crayons and pens with sparkly bits, before delving in deeper to bring out a Pac Man–shaped mini stapler, a cat pencil sharpener where the pencil went in an unfortunate place, and even a pack of dinosaur plasters.

"Mum made me pack those," Tom said, blushing.

Finally he found his special rubber and chucked it over.

The rubber took off half the page as well as my blobby writing. But I was still tempted to rub out the whole thing and start again. I might have if Miss Archibald hadn't started humming again.

"Ah good, good, I have your attention. I saw lots of you writing away and I'm very curious to hear how you've started your journals. Is there anyone who would like to talk about what they've written or even read a bit out?"

"I mean, I could. I suppose. If you want me too, I mean I don't have to but…"

Miss Archibald raised her hand to quieten Tom. "Go ahead," she said, smiling encouragingly.

Tom got to his feet and cleared his throat dramatically.

"My name is Tom Harris. Me and my mum and dad just moved from Glasgow to Dark Muir to look after my grandma. She owns six Eriskay ponies. They're one of the oldest types of horses and are very rare. They poop a lot though and adults can't ride them, so my dad wants to sell them and move back home. Grandma said over her dead body. But I don't think that's going to happen anytime soon, because it turns out she's pretty terrifying."

Blair sniggered and rolled her eyes. But Tom didn't look like he was about to stop talking.

"That's very nice," Miss Archibald said holding up a hand and cutting Tom short. "It sounds like you've got lots to write about this year."

I noticed that for all Tom's bravado his ears had turned bright red. I tried to catch his eye, but he was already busy arranging his many pens in order of colour and size.

"Now, I want you to keep your books safe because I'd like you to keep working on them all year," Miss

Archibald went on. "All right then, before we leave is there anyone else who feels confident to share what they've written?"

I tried to make myself as small as possible and look anywhere but at Miss Archibald. But Blair kicked the side of my chair as hard as she could and I let out a little squeaky sound.

"Amelia, is it? Well, let's hear what you've written." Miss Archibald smiled as if she wasn't completely mad and this was a totally normal thing to ask me.

Tom hadn't had problems reading stuff out, not like me. He probably didn't even need to be in STAR classes. Next week he would find out this was all a horrible mistake and would be in normal lessons with everyone else. I looked down at the words swimming all over the paper, took a deep breath and then stood up and started to read. But even from the first word, I knew it was going to be a disaster. I couldn't make the words stay still on the page. They bounced around and my hands got all sweaty and my tongue felt like it was made out of chewing gum and kept getting stuck to the roof of my mouth. And everything came out all horrible and jumbled. And after fifty thousand years I still hadn't managed to get halfway through the second sentence, so Miss Archibald finally stopped me. "That's great, Amelia, I think that gives us a good starting point to work from."

But I knew what she was really thinking. I knew what everyone was thinking as easily as if they had been chanting it.

*Stupid, Stupid, Stupid!*

I sank down into my chair as Miss Archibald droned on about our journal projects. But I couldn't listen any more. Blair was sniggering behind me and Tom hadn't looked at me since. He hadn't even asked for his rubber back. So much for being good at school and making loads of friends. I missed Mum so bad it made my stomach hurt.

# Chapter 5

On the ferry back, people were still pointing to where Serpent's Tooth Rock had been. Everyone was whispering about it. A little part of me wanted to go and talk to Tom and ask him about the Eriskay ponies and how he felt about moving to Dark Muir from a big city like Glasgow. But I couldn't, not after what had happened in class. So I went and hid under the lifeboats again and watched the horseshoe shape of Dark Muir get bigger and bigger.

I had never wanted to go home less. I knew Da would ask me about my first day. He would want to know how many new friends I had made and how all my lessons had gone. I couldn't bear to tell him how I hadn't known anything all day. That everything he and

Grandpa had taught me about the stars and strange sea creatures was totally useless. That everyone else knew proper stuff, like how to do equations without getting too many noughts on the end. And how to do science experiments without setting fire to yourself. I brushed a strand of slightly singed hair behind my ear. I really didn't want to tell him about how I had spent lunch alone in the girl's loos. But worst of all, I couldn't tell Da how I had been put into the STAR group for the very stupid.

I trudged through the harbour trying to ignore Blair and her awful friends sniggering at me. Maybe, just maybe, if I'd worn the right shoes, she wouldn't have started the whole day off by picking on me. On the way home I pulled the wellies off and threw them over a fence and into a bog. I watched them sink from view and thought about Serpent's Tooth Rock. It was weird it had disappeared right after my birthday. I couldn't help but wonder what had happened to it? And why its disappearance was making everyone on the island act so weird? Sometimes in the middle of winter when the days are so short you're hardly up before the sun has gone down again, people go a bit strange. Last winter, under a full moon, you could make out people running around naked in the dark. Grandpa had said it was ghosts, but I was pretty sure it was just the old couple who ran the post office. If anyone could explain what was going on now though, it would be him.

But by the time I arrived home, Grandpa was in full swing of coming up with new ways that he might "pop his clogs". This was his way of saying dying. Nowadays, he talked about this a lot. In fact, it was his favourite subject. He even came up with little lists I liked to call:

**Grandpa McLeod's Fabulous Ways to Pop his Clogs.**
- Lightning strike
- Quicksand
- Spontaneous combustion

Grandpa listed these off as I threw my bag on the kitchen table.

"Grandpa, you're going to live to a hundred and get your letter from the Queen," I said, remembering the article Da had read me about how the Queen sent everyone a special letter on their hundredth birthday.

"I just want to prepare you for the inevitable," Grandpa said darkly.

I could smell butter and bacon sizzling on the hob. I knew Da was making an extra-special effort because it had been my first day at school. But somehow that just made me feel worse.

"So... How was it?" Da asked, flipping something on the stove.

"It was fine," I said, quickly pulling off my dirty socks under the kitchen table and hiding them in my pocket. Pipi came over from her basket by the stove and licked my toes. I think it was her way of telling me she was sorry I'd had a bad day. Dogs are weird like that.

"Have you seen that the Serpent's Tooth Rock's gone?" I said, trying to change the subject.

"Mmm," Da mumbled, salting something. "Some sort of natural tidal phenomenon. Happens once every seventy years apparently."

But I thought of the faces of the Selkie swimmers. And what Tom and Grandpa had said. This felt bigger than just something to do with the tides.

"Anyway, I want to hear all about your very first day at school," Da said, turning around from the stove wearing the stupid floral pinny that used to be Nana's.

"It was fine," I lied.

"Your first day at school, the thing you've been talking about all summer, was just fine?" Da asked.

I shifted in my seat, looking to Pipi for help. But she was too busy nibbling at her tail.

"They put me in special classes," I said as I felt my lip wobble.

"Oh, Amelia, I'm sure it's just temporary, to get you caught up. I bet by the end of the year you'll be reading and writing just as well as everyone else."

I shook my head. Da just didn't understand. He never understood. How would I ever be able to keep up with all the other children when I couldn't even read in my head?

"If Mum was here she would understand and I wouldn't have to go to stupid school and everything would be better," I whispered under my breath.

Da's face fell as he put my plate down in front of me. He had made my favourite – bacon and mushroom frittata cut into a smiley face. It sat there looking up at me with its funny wobbly ketchup smile.

"Well I'm sorry I'm not Mum then," Da said as he pulled on his big gum boots and his duffle coat. Da has had lots of jobs ever since Mum left. So when he's not fishing or working down the pub, he works as a mobile mechanic.

"I've been asked to fix Mr Gerard's truck. I'll be back in a couple of hours. Remember Hettie and Penny said they would come over if you needed any help." He glanced at Grandpa worriedly.

Hettie and Penny were the old ladies who lived in the cottage down the hill. They both creeped me out. Not because they both smoked without their dentures in, but because Hettie had big golden eyes, the kind witches are meant to have. And she wore a big yellow brooch that matched. But it wasn't an ordinary kind of brooch; it had a bee in it. A real bee! When I was little my Mum used to tell me terrifying stories about Hettie and Penny turning insects into jewellery and stuffing birds to hang in their house. I don't think Mum liked them much. And they certainly didn't like Mum. It wasn't until she left that they started coming around. I think they were checking up on me, Da and Grandpa. But we didn't need checking up on. We were just fine the way we were.

Grandpa looked anxious after Da slammed the door behind him. He doesn't like people leaving. Sometimes I think it's because he's worried he'll forget who they are when they come back. So I put my arm around him.

"What are we watching?" Grandpa asked after I took him into the sitting room.

We squished on to the old leather couch in front of the fire and I turned the television on to our favourite wildlife programme. David Attenborough was talking about birds that used to live at the time of the dinosaurs. I was sort of hoping Mum's name might pop up at the end of the show in the credits. Sometimes I look for little signs of her. That way she doesn't feel like she's completely gone.

After we finished watching David Attenborough, I helped Grandpa up the narrow wooden stairs to his little room. His window had been left open and rain was pouring in. I pulled the window shut as the sound of thunder crackled around us.

"Do you hear that?" Grandpa said in a faraway voice. "It's beginning, Amelia, it's beginning."

"It's just a storm, Grandpa," I said as I helped him into bed.

I tucked Grandpa up and put a photo of Grandma that had been knocked over back by his bedside table, before going to my room across the hall.

In bed I couldn't shake Grandpa's warning or what had happened on my first day of school. So I pulled out *The Little Book of Lady Adventurers* and flicked through the pages. I stopped at one of my favourite pictures. It was of a woman in a red parka covered in ice sitting on a sled next to a huge black dog.

"Helen Thayer was the first woman to travel to the Magnetic North Pole alone. At fifty years old Helen travelled across 364 miles of snow and ice with only a part-wolf, part-Inuit husky dog she named Charlie. Together they fought off polar bears, camped in sub-zero temperatures and battled through fierce arctic storms to reach their goal. After their trip Charlie came to live with Helen in the US. Being an Inuit dog, Charlie had never seen a garden before and got to lie on the grass in the sunshine for the very first time," I read slowly to Pipi.

"What do you think about you and me going on an arctic adventure?" I said, scratching behind Pipi's floppy ears.

Pipi barked enthusiastically. But I didn't think we'd get far. Not when Pipi had to hide under the table when the washing machine was on. And not when just thinking about taking a ten-minute ferry ride across to Bridlebaine Academy gave me a stomach ache. Adventurers weren't meant to be scared of big waves, or reading out loud, and they definitely weren't meant to be scared of going to school. I looked at the picture of Helen and Charlie again, wishing I could be half as brave.

I heard Da come home a couple of hours later, first the rattle of the kitchen door, then big footsteps up the little wooden staircase until he paused at my bedroom door. I expected him to do what he always did: come in and sit on the end of my bed for a little bit and then leave the door cracked open when he left. But this time he just stood in the doorway. I could tell he wanted to talk, but I was still angry. Angry for sending me to a stupid new school, angry for never understanding why I got so stuck on things and for getting upset whenever I mentioned Mum. I turned over and pretended to be asleep. Da waited, his shadow stretching over my bedroom. I could tell he wanted to say something. It hung heavy in the air. And a little part of me desperately wanted to talk to him too, but I pulled my blanket tighter around me. Da sighed and clicked the door shut behind him.

Afterwards I lay in bed listening to the wind beating through the trees and the rolls of thunder. Grandpa was right: it didn't sound like a summer storm. It sounded like the start of something much bigger.

# chapter 6

It was midnight when it happened.

It wasn't the bolt of lightning that woke me up. Or the sound of Pipi's howling. Or even the strange mixed-up dream I'd been having about running through a forest surrounded by glowing stones searching for Mum. It was the tingling in my hand, the hand that had touched the Serpent's Tooth Rock. It was stronger than I had felt it on my birthday. And it wasn't just hot; it felt like it was on fire!

Then my room began to flicker. The glow-in-the-dark stars and streams of origami birds hanging from the ceiling shook and danced. I dived under the covers. This was all in my head. I was just imagining it. But then there was the sound of a wild storm, and it was closer than ever before, like I was outside in it. And then I was shimmering and flickering just like the room. I tried to cry out, but couldn't make a noise. I struggled to get up, to get Da, but as I looked down, my legs vanished. Pipi leaped in the air, barking like mad. Her little legs were running in the air, her floppy ears flapping up and down with each jump. I reached out to touch her but my hand, the hand that had touched the Serpent's Tooth Rock, disappeared. I reached out with my other hand and grabbed Pipi's collar as the roar of the wind got louder and louder.

The room flickered and whirled around me and *whoosh*.

I disappeared.

# chapter 7

When I opened my eyes, Pipi and I weren't in my bed any more. I wasn't even in my room. I was pretty sure I wasn't even in my house. Because it was no longer my glow-in-the-dark stars that twinkled above me. I was out under the big, bright night's sky.

The storm that had roared in my ears was suddenly all around me. It ripped through the tall trees and crackled through the sky. I tried to get to my feet, but my body was all wobbly, like I had just done a really long run. Gently, I sat up, the blood rushing to my head. I could hear the frantic beating of my heart. Pipi licked my face. She only does this when I'm sad or ill, but I wasn't either. I wasn't sure what I was. I felt all mixed up. What had just happened? And where was I?

All around me were standing stones. The same stones from the dream.

I must still be dreaming, I told myself. So I shut my eyes tight, feeling certain that at any moment I was going to wake up and I'd be back in my little room, tucked under my velvet blanket, listening to Grandpa snoring and the rattle of the loose catch on my window. But all I could hear was the roar of the wind as the rain soaked through my dinosaur pyjamas. And when I opened my eyes again, it wasn't my glow-in-the-dark stars that twinkled above me.

I reached out and touched the stones. They felt cold and hard and very real. And so did my frozen feet and wet pyjamas and Pipi's shaking body in my arms. This wasn't a dream. I balled my fists together and held my breath and hoped that whatever magic had taken me would take me back. Because I knew these stones; I knew this place. And it was the last place in the world I wanted to be! It was where everything had gone wrong on my ninth birthday.

It had all started off so brilliantly. Mum and Da hadn't argued all day and Grandpa had given me these amazing chess pieces that he'd carved out of wood. The knight was extra special because he'd made it look like a shaggy Shetland pony. But best of all, Mum had decided I was finally old enough to go camping with her. I could go anywhere on Dark Muir I wanted. And there was only one place I wanted to go: Sometimes Island. You can only reach it when the tide is low, so most of the time it's a secret island. It seemed such a magical place.

Mum had got me an Indiana Jones hat and a hiking backpack with pockets for everything. She even let me use her special binoculars, the ones her da gave her for her very first trip abroad. We had climbed a tree and taken turns with the binoculars to watch a nest of short-eared owls. Then we walked all the way to the top of the island and Mum had shown me the standing stones and explained how the stones were meant to be the scales flicked from the sea serpent's tail when it had churned the seas to make the islands. When it got dark we made a campfire and ate hotdogs and burnt marshmallows and Mum told me about her adventures filming clouded leopards in Borneo. It had been the first time in ages that Mum seemed really happy.

But I didn't like camping as much as I thought I would in the dark. I couldn't sleep with all the strange noises around me. And it was so dark in my tent without the glow of my plastic stars. And then something had slithered into my sleeping bag. It was warm and smooth and not at all like how you would imagine a snake to feel like. But that didn't make it any less terrifying as it slipped across my feet.

"Mum!" I screamed, furiously trying to wiggle out of my sleeping bag.

It took a moment for Mum to groggily open her eyes. But then she leaped into action, grabbing the snake by the tail and flinging it out the tent door.

"I got it. It's gone," she soothed.

But I couldn't stop panicking; imagining that my whole sleeping bag was filled with snakes. Or even worse: that my pyjamas were filled with snakes too.

"What if there's more!" I sobbed.

"I don't see any," Mum said, waving her torch across the tent.

The tent was filled with shadows and in my head all sorts of horrible things were hiding in the dark. I stood on one foot, refusing to get back into my sleeping bag.

"Amelia, come here," Mum said, pulling out *The Little Book of Lady Adventurers* that she'd packed for our trip.

"Remember Kate Jackson?" She flipped to a page with a picture of a woman in glasses grinning, her head covered in snakes.

"She was so scared the first time a snake crawled over her, that she wouldn't stop screaming. But then she went on to travel the world collecting snakes. She even went on an adventure to the Congo where she was bitten by one of the snakes she had found. Luckily it wasn't a venomous snake. But in surviving the bite her pygmy guides believed she was a witch," Mum told me.

"She wasn't, was she?" I asked.

Mum shook her head and carried on.

"The next time she got bitten she wasn't so lucky, though, because it was from the deadly black cobra." Mum waved her arm and turned her hand into the hungry mouth of a cobra. "But she managed to rush back to her camp and get the antivenom in the nick of time," Mum finished, snapping the book shut and putting her arm around me.

But for the first time, one of Mum's stories hadn't made me feel better. It had made me feel much, much worse. I couldn't stop imagining black cobras in every corner of the tent, waiting to slither into my sleeping bag and bite me.

"I want to go home!" I yelled.

"But I thought we were having such a good time, just us girls."

"Da wouldn't have let a snake crawl into my bed."

Mum's face fell. "I was trying so hard to make this nice," she said.

And it had been. It had been almost the perfect day, until I ruined it. In the morning Mum had packed up our rucksacks and our tent and we had gone home. She hadn't said a word about why we had to cut our trip short to Da. But I knew how disappointed she was in me.

A week later, Mum left. I knew it was all my fault. If I had just been braver that night everything could have been different.

The sky burst into rain. I fell back, shivering, and Pipi leaped into the air, snapping at the streaks of lightning. I'd landed on something hard and I turned to see something glinting in the ground. Half buried by dirt and leaves were Mum's binoculars! I turned them over in my hands; they felt as heavy and precious as the first time I'd held them. I frowned. Why hadn't Mum come back for them? She'd need them on her adventures all over the world, wouldn't she? The lightning crackled overhead. I put the leather strap around my neck and tried pretending I was one of Mum's favourite explorers, brave and fearless.

I tried to remember the way back home. But all I could recall was that it had been a long walk. What would Da think if he woke up to find me missing? He would be so mad when he found me. Then I shivered as a dark little thought crept into my head. What if he never found me? I got to my feet shakily. We couldn't stay here. My dinosaur pyjamas were already soaked through. And the storm was only getting worse.

"I don't suppose you know the way home?" I asked Pipi.

But before Pipi could reply, the trees rippled as if something very large was moving in them. An owl screeched, birds took off from the bushes, and then we heard it: a deep rumbling growl. Pipi looked up, sniffing the air. Then she bolted through the undergrowth.

"Wait!" I yelled after her.

But it was too late. I watched her white body dart into the trees and then I couldn't see her any more. I could only hear barking. I ran after her, calling her name. I didn't know where I was going. Everything looked strange and different in the dark. My feet slipped over wet grass and tripped over tree trunks, branches lashed out at my face and then I heard it again: the low growl. And then Pipi's barking stopped.

"Pipi!" I yelled. But there was nothing.

I could feel my imagination going to the dark little place in the back of my head. The place that comes up with all sorts of frightening things. I imagined the horrible fates that could have happened to Pipi. She could have fallen into a rock pool, or been attacked by mad owls, or eaten by hungry foxes.

"Please don't let Pipi have been eaten by foxes. Please let her be OK," I whispered.

The wind howled, and the night crackled with lightning. But from far away, I thought I heard a bark.

I ran towards it. My hands caught on thorns, the leg of my pyjamas ripped, and then my foot slipped and suddenly I was on my bum and sliding fast. I tried to grab on to tree branches, but they whipped through my hands. As I slid through the undergrowth, I could hear the barking again. But I couldn't see anything as I tumbled into the dark.

With a jolt I landed on something furry and growling. I was sure I had fallen right into the monster's waiting jaws, but then it licked my face.

"Pipi!" I yelled, and she buried her wet nose into me.

When I managed to pull Pipi off I could see we weren't by the standing stones any more. We weren't even in the forest. We had fallen on to a rocky bank.

"Where did you take us?" I said, scratching Pipi behind her ears.

The rain stopped as quickly as it had begun. The sky brightened and out from the trees I could see the slope of the cliffs and the lights of the harbour. And straight up, right above me, I could see the brightest star in the sky, lighting the way back to our house on the hill.

"You found it, Pipi, you found the way home!" I said, grabbing her front paws and dancing.

Even though my feet were cut and bruised, and I couldn't stop shivering, I started running towards the lights in the harbour. But before I could make it very far, Pipi grabbed on to my pyjama trousers. She growled and wouldn't let go.

"Look, it's no use being scared now," I said, shaking her off.

Pipi whimpered. She didn't agree.

"Come on," I said, "I can see our house. It's just a bit further, I promise."

But Pipi wouldn't move. She lay down and put her head in between her paws instead.

"Fine, then. We'll just live here. In the middle of nowhere, for ever, with scary animals that like to eat small children and their dogs. That sounds good to you?" I said, collapsing down next to her. Pipi licked my hand.

"We should've got a cat," I said, shaking my head.

I got up and starting walking towards home, sure Pipi would follow. But it didn't take me long to realize why she hadn't. I hadn't taken more than a few steps before there was a horrible eggy smell, then a rush of water, and with a slurp my foot disappeared. In the dark I hadn't seen that the way back home was across a deadly peat bog. I pulled my foot out, but the other one sank further in. I tried to dart across the next few steps. I was sure if I just ran fast enough I could make it. I stumbled over the bog, the mud squelching between my toes. But it wasn't long before I fell into another marshy spot. With a gurgle my ankle disappeared, and then my knee. I wiggled forward but every step made me sink faster. The mud bubbled and oozed and with a great slurp both my legs were pulled under. I could hear Pipi barking from the bank. But it was too late to turn back.

# chapter 8

The mud pulled me down further, my feet were numb and I was so tired, so very tired. If I just closed my eyes, if I just took a little rest…

I was alone in the dead of night being sucked under by a bog. But up ahead I could see something. Was it a large rock? A seaweed-covered island? Whatever it was, I had to get to it. I was nearly up to my waist and sinking fast. Think, think! I squeezed my eyes shut in concentration. The story of Beryl Markham popped into my head. Beryl Markham was the first woman to fly solo East to West across the Atlantic. But on her attempt to be the first person to fly nonstop from Europe to New York, her plane had crash-landed into a freezing bog in Nova Scotia.

I remembered Mum reading me her story and telling me what to do if I ever found myself in a bog. We even made a list and called it Beryl's Tips. It flooded back into my head.

**Beryl's tips to escape a Deadly Bog:**
1. Don't panic
2. Pretend you're swimming
3. Go slow

Tip number one was easy. I stopped thrashing about and the awful gurgling stopped. Tip number two was harder. How was I supposed to swim in mud? But I threw myself on to my belly, grabbed a mossy clump and pulled myself forward. Slurp. I felt my right leg pull out of the mud, just a bit. I wriggled forward, the bog oozing around me. But the mud no longer felt like a vice on my legs. With another shuffle forward my right leg came free and then the other slid out.

Tip number three was the hardest. I inched myself forward, half-crawling, and half-swimming through the smelly bog. But I was still sinking. My mouth was filling with oozy mud, my toes and my knees were being dragged beneath me. Inch by inch I pulled myself closer to the rocky island. Finally I grabbed hold of it and hoisted myself up. There was a sucking sound and then I was free! I scrambled up on to the rock, panting.

I looked around. There were three flat mossy mounds between me and the beach that led up to the cliff tops. If I could jump to each one of them, I could make it home. But I could hear Pipi still barking from the bank. There was no way she could make it through the mud to the rock island. And there was no way I was leaving her behind.

"Come on, Pipi, jump!" I yelled.

But Pipi just barked and ran up and down the bank.

"Jump!" I called out again in desperation, patting my muddy thighs and whistling.

I thought of all the tricks I had tried to teach her back home. When she was a puppy I tried to make her leap through a hoop, or climb up a slide, but I barely managed to make her understand the words "sit" and "stay" and I had only managed to do it then by promising her biscuits. Biscuits were the only thing that persuaded Pipi to do anything, I suddenly realized.

"Biscuits!" I yelled.

Suddenly a white furry shape was flying through the air. With a thump Pipi landed in my arms. I hugged her tight, letting her nuzzle into me, her wet nose pressing against my ear.

"I guess it's my turn now," I said, getting up and staring across to the other rock islands. I tucked Pipi into my pyjama top, wrapped my arms around her and with a deep breath I jumped. I could feel my legs cartwheeling through the air, Pipi slipping out from my arms, and then thud.

My feet landed on the rock and Pipi wriggled the rest of the way out of my shirt. I looked out at the final rock island. It was further away than the last jump and I had barely made this one. I couldn't carry Pipi with me this time. But Pipi didn't seem to want to get back into my pyjama top. She was already standing on the edge waiting for me.

"Together," I said, and Pipi barked in agreement.

We hurtled ourselves on to the last rock, panting. I clambered up the mossy top and slid down the other side to the beach. As soon as my feet touched solid ground I started yelling and Pipi joined in barking and spinning around in the sand, furiously wagging her tail. We were finally safe.

It was nearly dawn by the time Pipi and me could see our house, its white stone walls twinkling in the fading moonlight. I had never been so pleased to see it. I squeezed through the half-open back window and stood in the kitchen shivering and shaking. I pulled moss and twigs from my hair and brushed the dirt and leaves from my poor cut feet.

In the gloom of the kitchen I waited for Da or

Grandpa to rush down the stairs to wrap me in their arms, relieved to see me. I even waited for Da to storm into the kitchen, shake me by my shoulders and yell at me for disappearing in the middle of the night. But the house was quiet. All I could hear was the ticking of the clock and the racing of my heart. Nobody had noticed I was gone.

In my room I stuffed Mum's binoculars into the bottom shelf of my bedside drawer. Then I took off my dinosaur pyjamas. The mud coating them was so thick that it took both me and Pipi pulling at them before they came off. I bunged the trousers and the top deep into the back of my wardrobe. In the bathroom, as I washed off the rest of the dirt and pulled on a fresh pair of pyjamas, I looked at myself in the mirror. There was a little cut across my cheek. But I couldn't remember how it had happened. I couldn't remember very much at all. I tried to remind myself, but I was so tired and it all sounded so impossible.

When I went back to my room, Pipi was asleep on the foot of my bed. The storm had faded away and it was as if nothing had happened. I climbed into bed and wrapped my velvet blanket around me. Maybe when I woke up tomorrow this was all going to have been a horrible nightmare, I thought, before sleep closed in around me.

# Chapter 9

After Mum left I put all the things I didn't want to think about into a box in my head. But the problem with this is sooner or later the box gets so full up that all the scary and nasty thoughts come pouring out. When that happened I got really upset and did all sorts of bad things. Like I'd smashed up all my space shuttle models and once I'd even tried to run away. But running away when you live on a tiny island is difficult: it's not like you can get very far. So it hadn't been very hard for Da to find me after an hour or so, sitting on the bench outside the post office. I thought he was going to be so cross with me. But he wasn't. He'd just wrapped me up in his arms and cried. I'd never seen Da cry before, so I'd started crying too.

That's when Da made me promise to talk to him about the things that upset me.

But I didn't know how to tell him about last night. I wasn't even sure what had happened. One moment I had been in my room and then poof, I'd disappeared and ended up on Sometimes Island. All I knew was it was something to do with the Serpent's Tooth Rock. The day I had touched it, it had made something happen to me.

"Da, do you think you can be cursed?" I asked over my bowl of cornflakes the next morning.

Grandpa's porridge spoon clattered on to the floor. Da just sighed.

"No, Amelia, I do not."

"I think Grandpa's right. I think the rock did something to me," I said.

Da poured a big cup of coffee. The kind of cup of coffee that meant he had a long day ahead and he was definitely not in the mood for this conversation.

"Let me guess, you're ill with something horrible like…" Da paused, searching for the right word.

"Bubonic plague," Grandpa added helpfully.

"And you can't go to school?" Da finished.

"No, I'm not ill, it's much worse!" I began, but Da was having none of it.

"I know you had a bad start to school. But you can't

just give up after one day. I need you to try. Because, Amelia, we can't go back to the way things were."

I opened my mouth again. But none of the right words came out. In fact, no words came out at all. I didn't know how to explain what had happened. Even I half didn't believe it. But I could feel my head throbbing with everything. I had to tell someone. And there was only one person I could think of who would understand.

That night, before I went to bed, I pulled out Miss Archibald's blue book from my bag.

Dear Mum, I wrote.

Here are all the people I know who have disappeared:

- Peng Jiamu, 55, a Chinese biologist who disappeared in a desert. Some say he found a lost temple, others say he vanished in a sandstorm.
- Percy Fawcett, 58, went into the Amazon jungle never to return. Possibly eaten by jaguars.
- Amelia Earhart, 39, my namesake, who disappeared trying to fly solo across the globe.

And me, Mum. Last night I disappeared. I don't know how or why and no one will believe me. I don't even know if it will happen again.

# chapter 10

I hadn't tried to talk to Da or Grandpa again about the disappearing. Too much else had happened. A week of school had gone by in a blur of tests, strange science experiments and STAR lessons. I still hadn't got used to going to classes either; sitting still in a classroom for hours at a time felt almost impossible. At home I had always been able to go and grab a snack, or pop to the loo, and when the weather was good Mum and Grandpa had taken me outside to do classwork.

But having proper classrooms wasn't all bad. The art room was a bit magic. It was filled with huge paintings and sculptures that the year elevens were working on, with a wall rack filled with every colour of paint you could imagine. I'd ended up getting a bit carried away using them all on my self-portrait. My art teacher, Miss Iris, had said my picture was "very experimental". I wasn't sure if that meant it was good or bad. This was something I'd learned about teachers: they never said what they really thought. Well, apart from our drama teacher, Mr Todd, who believes in expressing yourself. He started every lesson with us roaring like lions and had begun teaching us a dance that involved a lot of stomping. Tom was terrible. He kept waving his arms at the wrong time and tripping over his feet; Mr Todd had to make him his deputy choreographer just to keep everyone safe. But the rest of my lessons weren't so fun. Our science teacher, Mr McNair, spoke in long sentences that never seemed to end, and in English we were studying Shakespeare. This seemed doubly unfair when I struggled with regular words, let alone grand Shakespearian ones. Miss Archibald sat next to me in these classes to help explain things and make notes. But this made it hard to make friends, because nobody wanted to sit next to a teacher. School was so much to take in that it was almost enough to make me forget about the night I'd disappeared. Well, almost…

"Amelia!" Miss Archibald bellowed.

I looked up from my journal. It was our Monday morning STAR class and Miss Archibald was staring down at me and flapping her arms, looking even more like a surprised owl than ever.

"I think this is the third time I've asked how your journal writing is going," Miss Archibald said.

"She's probably daydreaming again," Blair hissed, curling her lip.

Blair was right; I did daydream. I didn't mean to do it. But sometimes I ended up thinking about how fast a cricket's heart beats, or if you never cut your fingernails would they keep growing and growing until they became long curly claws and you couldn't lift your hands up, or if you were to climb Mount Everest with a beard would it get all frozen and turn into a block of ice? But this time I was thinking about the night I had nearly drowned in the bog. How it had been one week today since I disappeared.

Nothing strange had happened since. Even Grandpa seemed to have stopped predicting impending doom. And looking back over what I had written to Mum, it all seemed so ridiculous. Was I sure I had disappeared? Had Beryl Markham really helped me get out of a deadly bog? Was I sure it hadn't just been a strange dream? All these questions made my head spin. Maybe it would be better if I forgot about it. I slammed the blue exercise book shut and Miss Archibald raised an eyebrow.

"You know it's OK to not let me see what you're writing, Amelia. It's your journal project and that means it can be private. I just wanted to check after last week to see if you needed any more help."

I shook my head.

"All right then, Miss Chatterbox," Miss Archibald grinned. "Right, class, you can put your journals away. We won't be writing them during lessons any more. They're something for you to do at home."

"Like homework?" Gregory asked.

"Yes, I suppose so," Miss Archibald replied.

"So does that mean we get out of doing our other homework then?" Ian shouted.

"Sadly, it does not," Miss Archibald said. "But there is the chance to get a very special prize for it at the end of the year."

"A prize like not having to do any homework?" Gregory grinned.

"I'm about to give you extra in a moment, Gregory Wilson. Now, everyone turn your attention to the board. Today we will be studying punctuation."

Everyone groaned and shoved their blue books into their bags. I glimpsed a flash of Tom's journal before it disappeared. I could see it was filled with the most amazing pictures of ponies. He had even coloured them in with shading to make them look 3D.

I didn't think that's what Miss Archibald had in mind when she set us a writing exercise, but I thought Tom's drawings were brilliant. I wanted to go over and ask for a closer look, but I could see Blair glaring at me and Miss Archibald was in full swing, telling us something very boring about commas.

The rest of the lesson crawled by and the school day felt like it would go on for ever. Finally, the last bell went and we were heading back home. I sat on the bus on my own again, but on the ferry Tom came over.

"Hey," he said, sitting down on the empty seat next to me.

"Hey," I replied.

Tom drummed his leg nervously against the chair.

"So I've been meaning to ask…" Tom paused. "If I could have my rubber back."

"Sure," I said, digging around in my bag and pulling the rubber out from my pencil case.

"Great, thanks, cheers, that's brilliant," Tom said, getting up and stuffing the rubber into his pocket and walking off. But he hadn't got more than a few paces away when he turned back around.

"Actually I didn't really need the rubber back. I've got about ten of them at home; I just wanted an excuse to talk to you. I've been trying to talk to you all week, but I felt a bit embarrassed after what had happened in that first STAR class."

"Oh," I said, flashing back to how horrible it had been trying to read out loud in class for the first time.

"I can read!" I said flushing bright red all over again. "It just takes me longer and in front of everyone I … couldn't do it," I finished lamely.

"No, Amelia, it wasn't anything you did," Tom interrupted me. "It was me! I was embarrassed. I made an idiot of myself reading out my journal. I just went on and on, until Blair started laughing and Miss Archibald made me stop. I thought I'd be all right if I was reading something I'd written down, but once I started, there just seemed to be more and more words," he said breathlessly. "Honestly, I wish I had your problem. Because I've got the opposite – I've got word vomit!"

I'd watched Tom throwing himself head first into everything all week. He'd even refused to give up learning Mr Todd's dance until he nearly knocked out Chloe. I'd thought he was kind of indestructible. But it turned out he was just as worried about school as me. It made me like him even more.

"I guess we're both idiots," I said.

Tom grinned.

"Yeah, best we stick together."

The ferry docked at Dark Muir and everyone streamed off still huddled in their special friendship groups. But for once I wasn't alone.

Me and Tom walked through the hodge-podge of harbour houses.

"So I guess I'll see you at school tomorrow?" Tom said when we got to my turning for Hartleroot hill.

I nodded, my belly feeling full of happy sparkles.

But this feeling didn't last long. As soon as I got home I knew something was wrong. The back door was wide open and Grandpa was nowhere to be found. I looked for him in the kitchen and then his bedroom. I even popped my head around the door of the scary little attic room. But there was no sign of him and Da wasn't home yet. This wasn't good.

Pipi was asleep in her basket, snoring as usual.

"Some watchdog you are," I said.

Pipi yawned and one of her ears flopped over her eyes. She hadn't been getting much sleep either. Ever since the night I disappeared, she wouldn't let me out of her sight. She would sit at the bottom of my bed keeping guard. Every time I got up she followed me, growling. Even when I went to the bathroom!

I sat down at the kitchen table and tried to think of all the places Grandpa would wander off to. But I didn't have to think for long because I could hear his voice coming up the path.

"Unhand me, woman," I heard Grandpa shout, and then Hettie and Penny, our thousand-year-old neighbours, appeared. Hettie had one of Grandpa's arms and Penny had the other and they were frogmarching him back to our house.

"Look who we found," Hettie said.

"I think he got a bit lost again," Penny joined in.

"Grandpa, you're not meant to go out without me and Da," I said, taking his arm and leading him into the kitchen. Hettie and Penny followed me in, keeping a wary eye on Grandpa just in case he attempted another great escape.

"I went to the shops. Can't a man go to the shops? But they moved everything. The post office wasn't where it was meant to be," Grandpa said.

"We all lose our way sometimes. No harm done," Penny said, her voice low and soothing.

"I did not get lost. I'm telling you, the post office was in the wrong place," Grandpa roared, and he went off to have a sulk in his chair.

"We found him down at the harbour," Hettie told me.

"I'm sorry," I said. "He's usually not too bad. But sometimes he gets a bit mixed up."

"Oh, don't you worry now. I think all us older people are a little off-balance since the rock disappeared…" Penny said, her voice trailing off.

"I never thought it would happen again in my lifetime," Hettie said darkly.

"We don't know this is the same thing," Penny said, shaking her head. "It could just be a high tide like the weather reported."

"You and me both know that's not true," snapped Hettie.

Pipi barked and spun around like she knew what they were talking about.

"It was your birthday the day before the rock disappeared, wasn't it, Amelia?" Hettie asked, her strange yellow eyes fixing on to mine and her bee brooch glinting in the sunlight.

I nodded, wanting desperately for them to leave. I didn't like where this conversation was going. I had only just managed to convince myself to forget about the strange night I had disappeared.

"Did you make a wish?" Hettie asked.

"I don't believe in wishes," I said boldly, trying not to think about how I'd asked the Serpent's Tooth Rock to help me find my mum.

"That's just as well, because dangerous things happen to those who are foolish enough to make wishes on Serpent's Tooth Rock."

"Leave the girl alone, you're scaring her," Penny said, putting a hand firmly on Hettie's shoulder. "Don't listen to any of that nonsense, Amelia. It's just folk tales and fancy. Hettie's got carried away, haven't you?"

But Hettie kept staring at me with her strange yellow eyes. I could tell she wanted to say something else. She opened her mouth and Penny swatted at her.

"You're right, it's probably nothing. Just the ramblings of an old lady," Hettie said, taking Penny's arm to leave. But before she did she gave me a stiff sort of smile that didn't reach her eyes.

I watched Hettie and Penny bickering on their way back down the hill. As scary as Hettie was, I had never once seen her argue with Penny. That was the one nice thing about them: they always seemed so happy together. But ever since the rock had disappeared, things seemed to be changing.

Later, in my bedroom, I couldn't stop thinking about what Hettie had said.

*Dangerous things happen to those who are foolish enough to make wishes.*

She couldn't be talking about me? Could she? A whole week had gone by and nothing bad had happened. I definitely hadn't disappeared again. I wasn't even sure it had happened the first time. It could have all been a bad dream brought on by a horrible first day at school. Da always said I had an overactive imagination.

"You heard what Penny said – Hettie's just trying to scare me. It's all an old wives' tale," I said out loud.

Pipi barked and began scratching at my bottom bedside table drawer. The drawer which I suddenly remembered I'd hidden the binoculars in the night I'd disappeared.

I pulled out my drawer, hoping against hope it would be empty. But the binoculars were there, still covered in mud. I picked them up and my hand began to tingle again, but so faintly I could tell myself it was just my imagination. Nothing strange was happening to me, I tried to tell myself again. But this time I wasn't so sure.

# Chapter 11

I tried to forget about Hettie's strange words. I even tried to forget about the disappearing. But just before the half-term holiday, it happened again.

It started with the fight. Just to make it clear, I wasn't the one who started it. In fact, I had been trying really hard to keep my promise to Da and try my best at school. But there are some things you just can't plan for. And one of them was Blair Watson.

We had to sit together again in geography because sometimes we got special help in class. Miss Archibald was helping us make notes and Miss Taylor, probably the oldest women alive, was talking about explorers who had accidentally discovered countries. It was a really interesting lesson, but I already knew most of it.

"Does anyone know who was the first European to discover America?"

I knew the answer but I was too afraid to stick up my hand.

"Christopher Columbus," Blair shouted.

"That's a good answer. But it's actually not true. Does anyone else know?"

"Leif Eriksson," I whispered under my breath.

"Go on," Miss Archibald said, and she poked me in the ribs.

"Amelia, do you know?" Miss Taylor asked.

"A group of Vikings led by the daring Leif Eriksson found America and set up a settlement about five-hundred years before Columbus," I said.

Miss Taylor clapped her hands.

"Well, I've never had someone get that right before. I think that deserves a house point."

"I didn't know you knew so much about explorers, Amelia," Miss Archibald beamed.

It was the first time a teacher had ever seemed pleasantly surprised by something I had said in class. I felt a warm glow of pride, like I had swallowed sunshine.

"Teacher's pet," Blair whispered under her breath.

And just like that my summer's-day-feeling went away.

"That's enough, Blair; do you want to get another detention?" Miss Archibald said.

I wished right then I had never answered the stupid question because I saw Blair glare at me under her fringe. I knew that look. That was the look of a very mad girl plotting something especially mad just for me.

Miss Archibald kept a close eye on me and Blair until the break bell rang. Then everyone went screaming into the corridors. I waited behind until the classroom was empty and tried to sneak out. But Blair was waiting for me outside, a massive pair of scissors in her hands. I tried to run but as I turned around I heard a loud *snip*. I felt for my hair but it was still there. Blair had cut a hole in my backpack instead. My books tipped out on to the ground. Her cronies – a girl called Grace and a pair of redheaded sisters – started laughing.

"Leave her alone," I heard Tom shout.

"Aw, isn't that sweet, you got a boyfriend," Blair laughed, picking her way through my books. "Oh, what do we have here," she yelled, waving my *Little Book of Lady Adventurers* around. I'd been carrying it in my bag ever since the first day of school. Somehow it made me feel safe, like it could prepare me for anything. But in Blair's hands it looked like nothing more than a scruffy old picture book.

"Oh my God, its baby's first picture book. Is this all you can read?" Blair snorted.

"Give it back," I said, trying to sound fierce.

"Or … what?" Blair replied, clearly enjoying herself.

Then with a loud rip she tore the first page out. I watched it flutter to the ground.

"Stop it!" I cried out.

But with a horrible twist of her lip Blair tore through another page and then another. Amelia Earhart flew through the air. Lady Hester Stanhope crumpled to the floor, the picture of her riding her Arab stallion trampled under Blair's big, fat foot.

I couldn't watch another page get destroyed. I clenched my fists and before I knew it I was hurling myself at Blair. I didn't think about the fact that she was twice as big as me. I didn't think about the fact that I was about to attack the scariest girl in school. Because the storm had come. The one that happened when I get really angry. It's like there was thunder in my belly and lightning in my fingertips and nothing and no one could stop me.

*Thump.*

Blair tumbled backwards, hit the wall and then plummeted into the lockers. There was a huge crashing sound, like a really big tree falling in the forest. Then the whole corridor went deathly quiet. The boys stopped messing about with their football. The girls stopped chatting. You didn't push Blair. You didn't even look at Blair if you could help it. Blair fixed me with a dark stare and then, the worst thing of all, she smiled the most terrifying smile I'd ever seen.

Then she began thumping every locker on her way towards me.

*Bash. Bash. BASH.*

Everyone in the corridor scattered, apart from me and Tom. We were both rooted to the spot. I could still feel the anger swirling through me, the way the wind rattles through open windows and doors into an empty house. But it was mixed up with pain too. Because *The Little Book of Lady Adventurers* lay in pieces. Blair had destroyed mine and Mum's special book. All our stories flew around the windy corridor. I wondered what Mum would have said if she had seen this. Suddenly my hand grew very hot.

"That was a mistake," Blair said, as she flicked her long ponytail over her shoulder.

With one swift movement she grabbed my shirt collar. I closed my eyes and braced myself for whatever awful thing was about to happen to me next, but suddenly there was a high-pitched scream. I opened my eyes. Blair was on the floor, her mouth wide open.

"What are you doing?" Blair said, pointing a shaking hand at me.

I looked down: my legs had disappeared! I blinked. I had to be imagining it. I just had to. But I could see the fear in Blair's eyes. All I could think was, *Not again, not again. This can't be happening again!* The corridor flickered in front of me. I tried to grab hold of something, anything. But it was too late. I could hear Tom shout, but his voice was really far away. The sound of thunder filled my ears and everything went dark.

When I opened my eyes, I was in a place I'd never been before. A place where no girl should ever go. I was lying flat out on the floor of the boys' toilets.

The boys' toilets, it turned out, were not like girls' toilets. They were a whole new world of disgusting. The ceiling was dotted with dried tissue balls and the whole room smelled very strongly of wee. This was worrying since I was lying in a large pool of something; something I very much hoped was water. I watched my legs flicker and then return but when I tried to get up I couldn't. The wind had been knocked out of me. I felt like I'd fallen from the sky and crash-landed on the floor. Outside I could hear shouting from the field and the smack of a ball hitting the window, so I knew the break bell hadn't rung yet.

Lying on the floor, I could hear the gentle splat, splat, splat of rain hitting the window. Then all of a sudden the sky opened up and I heard everyone on the field screaming and running inside from the unexpected downpour. I would have a very hard time explaining what I was doing lying on the floor if anyone came into the boys' loos. As I scrambled up, I groaned as I realized I would need to face Blair Watson, who had very much witnessed me evaporating into thin air.

# Chapter 12

Outside the boys' loos something caught my eye. In the centre of a dirty display case with a banner reading *Treasures of the Islands* was what looked like Mum's ammonite fossil. But it couldn't be, could it? I pressed my nose up to the glass and swiped a layer of dust away with my blazer sleeve. There it was, Mum's purple shell fossil, the one that I'd thought was sitting in a drawer at home. I would never have spotted it if I hadn't come out of the boys' toilet into an empty corridor. I leaned over the case to take another look and the door creaked open. I looked around and then reached in. I held it in my hands like it was something very precious, because this was Mum's treasure. The reason she had met Da.

Mum had loved telling me the story. How she had come to the islands to see the puffins but ended up finding love instead. I made sick noises when she said that bit. But she would carry on telling me how she had been down on the beach and found this amazing purple shell.

"I'd never found a fossil before," Mum would say. "So once I found one, I wanted to find another. I thought maybe this cave was filled with them. So I decided to go exploring. I was so busy searching that I didn't notice the tide coming in. By the time I'd felt my socks getting a bit wet, it was too late. The beach had disappeared under the waves and I was stranded. I thought all my adventures had come to an end."

And then Mum would do this big dramatic pause, even though we both knew what happened next.

"But then I saw this yellow boat. I started screaming but the man sailing it couldn't hear me. I waved my arms around but he couldn't see me. And then the boat started to move away. So there was nothing left for it. I dived into the sea. The water was so cold. And for a moment my whole body froze. But I could see that yellow boat and that man. So I kicked. And then I kicked again. And the boat got a little closer and closer still, until I could grab the side. And with all my strength I managed to pull myself in. And guess who was in the boat?" Mum would ask, and I would always pretend not to know the answer.

"Your da! And he was so surprised to see a woman covered in seaweed in his boat that he thought I was a mermaid," Mum had always finished.

I looked down at the ammonite and remembered how it had sat on top of the fireplace in the living room. Until Mum had said it was too fragile and had hidden it away in a drawer.

I turned the fossil over. There was a sticker on it that read: *Kindly donated by Ewan McLeod*. I couldn't believe Da had given this away! He knew I loved it just as much as Mum did. He'd even let me borrow it once. It was the night Mum had left for her filming job. The night she left and never came back. I hadn't been able to sleep, so Da had given me the fossil so I wouldn't miss her as much. Then he had dressed me up like a mermaid in a green bath towel and an old Halloween wig and told me stories about selkies under the sea until I'd fallen asleep.

"Shouldn't you be in class, Amelia?" Miss Rutherford said, suddenly appearing from around the corner. I slipped the ammonite into my pocket and dashed down the empty corridor.

## chapter 13

I knew I was super late for class before I even turned the doorknob. I'd spent too long looking at the ammonite and it had taken me ages to find the science lab from the loos. So I was planning on sneaking in and slipping onto a chair at the back. Fat chance of that happening. As soon as I walked in I tripped over someone's bag and fell flat on my face. The whole class roared with laughter, everyone but Blair, who looked like she had just seen a ghost. Then Gregory started clapping and Mr McNair looked up from his desk and pointed sternly to the clock. As I struggled back to my feet I saw Tom trying to catch my attention. He didn't call me over or anything, or wave his hand in the air. Instead, he was making all kinds of crazy faces and shifting his eyes repeatedly to the seat next to him. But I didn't want to talk about what had happened. I just wanted to get on with our boring science work and wait for the day to be over.

But Mr McNair wasn't the kind of teacher to just let you work quietly through a textbook. Mr McNair liked to get everyone involved in one of his experiments. And that afternoon he had decided to do an experiment with bubbles. When he asked for a volunteer, everyone's hands shot up, apart from mine. Finally, Mr McNair picked Chloe. Then he covered her hands in special methane bubbles and lit them on fire. There was a quick burst of flame, Chloe squeaked, and then the bubbles disappeared and so did the flame. Chloe lifted her hands up and waved them around and everyone clapped. But I wasn't really watching any of it.

I kept thinking about what had happened. I had disappeared: there was no denying it, no trying to convince myself it was a dream, or even a nightmare. It was real and it was happening to me. My stomach churned; it felt like it was full of thunder and lightning.

"Are you OK, Amelia?" Mr McNair asked.

I shook my head. I thought I was going to be sick, sick all over my desk, all over horrible Blair. But even if I had thrown up everywhere it still would have only been the second worst thing to happen to me that day.

"Feel ill," I finally managed to squeak out.

Mr McNair nodded his head.

"Yes, you don't look well. Better go and see the nurse."

Tom pounced out of his seat, banging his knee in the process.

"I should go with her, sir," he said, rubbing his knee.

Mr McNair raised an eyebrow.

"You know … just in case," Tom added theatrically.

*Just in case of what?* I wondered. Just in case I disappeared again. I was already starting to miss back when I was scared of starting school, mortified at having to do special classes and terrified of the school bully. At least these were all normal things to be worried about.

"All right then, Tom, you can take Amelia to the nurse, but you're to come straight back," Mr McNair said, shooing us off.

I was halfway down the hall when I really was sick, all over Tom's shoes. I rushed into the girls' toilets. Tom followed me in sheepishly.

"Are you OK?" he called from the door.

"Fine," I said, curled over the toilet bowl. Thinking that maybe everything would be all right if I just stayed in here for ever.

"Do you want to talk about what happened earlier?" Tom asked.

"No," I yelled back, hunched over the toilet bowl, waiting to be sick again.

"I got your book by the way."

I groaned, thinking of the mess Blair had made of *The Little Book of Lady Adventurers*.

"It's not as bad as you think. I picked up most of the pages after you went and disappeared," Tom said.

"WHAT?" I yelled, hurling myself out of the toilet stall.

I had been so busy worrying about Blair I hadn't even thought about how I might explain everything to Tom. How could this day get any worse?

"Yeah, I think you might even be able to glue it back together," Tom said.

"Not that bit! The other thing," I whispered.

"Oh, yeah – the disappearing. That was pretty freaky! I mean, it looked like you just vanished. But you couldn't have, could you? Unless you're some sort of superhero? Did you get bitten by a radioactive spider, or are you genetically engineered? Or were you sent from another planet? Or maybe you're just really good at magic? My uncle made a mouse appear out of his coat for me once. He must have kept it in his pockets for ages because I only used to visit once a month—"

"Tom, stop!" I yelled.

"Oh right, sorry. Are you going to be sick again? Do you need me to hold your hair or something?"

"I don't do magic, all right?"

"Come on, you can tell me how you did it. I mean, you were sick on my shoes, I'm pretty sure that makes us best friends," Tom said.

Tom made a good point. I had thrown up on him and he hadn't run away screaming. Instead he was standing in the girls' loos, offering to hold my hair back.

"Can you keep a secret?" I asked.

Tom nodded.

So I took a deep breath and started to tell Tom the truth. Well, most of it. I told him about touching Serpent's Tooth Rock and the night I disappeared and even about Hettie and Penny's warning. I told him because I was scared and I needed to tell someone. But mostly, it was because out of all the people I knew, I wanted Tom as my friend.

Dear Mum,

Since I really have started disappearing, I think it's time I told you a bit more about it. So here's what I call:

**Six Things You Should Know about Disappearing**

1. If you disappear from one place you reappear somewhere else.

101

2. It happens when my hand starts to tingle, which I first felt when I touched Serpent's Tooth Rock.

3. It doesn't happen all at once. Legs seem to disappear first.

4. Whatever you have on you, you take with you.

5. After you disappear, it takes a moment of flickering before everything comes back. It's what I like to call the jelly stage. Imagine you are a giant jellyfish. Jellyfish have no bones and out of water they are just a gooey lump. This is what it feels like when you reappear.

6. Did you know animals can sense storms coming? Like horses have been known to stampede before a tornado, and birds to all fly away before a big storm hits. Well, my dog Pipi knows when I'm about to disappear. So if you suddenly get animals acting really weird around you, look out. Because something big and incredible and absolutely terrifying is probably about to happen to you.

I know this sounds pretty frightening. But I don't want you to worry too much, Mum, because I'm working on how to stop it. In fact, my new friend Tom has a plan.

# Chapter 14

So Tom's great idea was to use the internet to look up what was happening to me. All right, I admit, it wasn't the best plan. But it was a start. And it felt so good to have someone to finally talk to about all the crazy stuff that was happening to me that I didn't really mind that step one of Tom's master plan was to use Google.

Tom came round my house the first weekend of the half-term holiday to put our plan into action. Da was thrilled that for the first time in ages I had a friend round. He didn't even seem to mind that there was a boy in my room, or that every time he popped up, we not so subtly hid the search results for things like:

- How to stop disappearing
- How to know if you've been cursed
- What is the likelihood of waking up with superpowers (that was Tom's idea)

In fact, Da wouldn't stop coming up to offer us home-made biscuits and tea and even a strange brown drink he found at the bottom of the cupboard. Tom was so polite that he even tried a bit, and then promptly spat it out.

"Eurgh, it's like drinking a beefburger," Tom said after Da left. "Want some?"

"Strangely enough, no," I said, laughing.

"Your da seems nice though," Tom said. "Have you tried to tell him about your little problem?"

This is what Tom called the whole disappearing thing. It didn't seem like a little problem, it seemed like a pretty gigantic one. I hadn't tried to tell Da again, or even Grandpa. I shook my head.

"I just don't know how you can keep something this big to yourself," Tom said, giving "How not to disappear" another Google. Lots of self-help websites came up, but none of it was useful.

"Well, I haven't; you know now. Oh, and I guess Blair does too..."

"Probably best to try not to think about that too

much," Tom shuddered.

But it was hard not to. I had seen her face in science class. I knew this was something she wasn't going to forget. It would almost have been better if she had just punched me, because I felt sure that whatever she was lying in wait and plotting would be so much worse.

"This is no good," Tom said, scrolling through another website offering advice on how to get incredible vanishing waistlines.

"How about looking up Serpent's Tooth Rock?" I said, and Tom typed it in.

10,032 hits.

We scrolled through a page, but it was mostly just pictures and a report of some tourist who fell off whilst trying to climb it. But when we got to the bottom of the second page there was something interesting.

*Myths, Legends and the Curse of Serpent's Tooth Rock.*

The page took ages to load. Internet and phone signal can be really dodgy on the island, which is why Da refused to get me a phone, even though everyone else had one. As the loading circle was spinning away I thought about telling Tom the one thing I had left out of my story: what I had wished for on Serpent's Tooth Rock. I worried if I told Tom about Mum and how she had left, it would change everything. I remembered how everyone had acted when they found out. No one knew quite what to do or say around me. Even Chloe, who had been my friend, acted really odd. It made me so angry that I ended up being really mean to her. It had ruined our friendship and I didn't want that to happen with me and Tom.

Finally the page loaded and I heard a little gasp from Tom.

*The Myth of Serpent's Tooth Rock*

I felt a shiver down my spine, like I already knew what it would say. I squinted and traced each letter with my finger, mouthing the words slowly.

One of the main landmarks of the small fishing island of Dark Muir, Serpent's Tooth Rock is meant to bring both good and bad luck to the islanders. When the rock is above water it shows the weather is fair, however if the rock is low in the water a big storm is due.

That explained why everyone on Dark Muir seemed so worried. I had been little when a big storm last hit and that had destroyed half the harbour boats. But it was nothing compared to the storm Grandpa lived through when he was a little boy. The island nearly had to be evacuated. But all this still didn't explain the disappearing or Hettie's strange warning.

Serpent's Tooth Rock has long also been thought to have magical powers, rumoured to grant both wishes and curses. For centuries islanders have held the rite of passage of touching the rock on their eleventh birthday.

"Did you read it?" Tom asked.

I nodded. I'd struggled with some of the words, but I understood enough. The rock couldn't have possibly granted my wish. It had cursed me, just like Grandpa said.

"Is that it? Isn't there anything on how to stop it?"

Tom shook his head.

"Oh, wait," Tom said. "For more information check out the following book: *Illustrated Myths of Dark Muir* by Hugo Bottomly and Florence Fields. That's our next clue!"

"A book?" I said. "There's Mr Sinclair's bookshop in the harbour but I haven't been there in ages."

I didn't want to tell Tom I had stopped going when I had grown too old to look at the picture books.

"Oh, I know that shop!" Tom said, bouncing up and down. "My gran took me there a couple of weeks ago. It has all these really old spooky-looking books. It's bound to have this one!"

That was the great thing about Tom; he made everything sound so easy. Find the book, stop the disappearing. That was the plan anyway, before everything went spectacularly and very terribly wrong.

# Chapter 15

I had a weird twisting feeling in my stomach as me and Tom walked down the hill to the harbour shops. Would this book solve the puzzle of my disappearing? And if it did, would Tom no longer be interested in being my friend? Hanging out with him had been the best thing to happen to me in such a long time. Yesterday we had spent time exploring the tiny island – I had shown Tom my favourite areas and Tom had shown me his. We had gone treasure hunting in the caves at Smugglers Beach, visited the seals at Hope Cove and hung out at Tom's grandma's farm. We had even named the new ponies together. And I hadn't disappeared once.

When we got to the bookshop our excitement fizzled out when we spotted the big *Closed for renovations* sign across the door. Tom jiggled the gold handle on the door and I peered in through the dusty window into the darkness inside. I could just about make out white sheets covering all the bookcases.

Tom was distraught. "Gran and I were just here the other day! I tried not to laugh when I saw her buying all these embarrassing romance novels. And right at the back there's all these really cool old books that you're not meant to touch, but I couldn't help it and then Gran told me off and said she couldn't take me anywhere. And I was scared she was going to get really mad with me. You wouldn't know it because she's really small, but she can be absolutely terrifying when she gets cross. But it was all right in the end because she calmed down and bought me a book about drawing comics."

I could tell Tom was upset because he couldn't stop talking.

"We should have come here sooner. I'm so sorry, Amelia," he said miserably.

"There might be another way in," I said, pointing to the half-open window on the first floor of the shop.

"You can disappear, Amelia, not fly," Tom said.

"I won't need to," I replied, peering around the side of the bookshop where a spindly tree was growing up around some very thick, spiky-looking holly bushes.

Our plan was as follows:
- Climb the tree, careful not to fall into the holly bush of death
- Sneak through the unlocked top window
- Find *Illustrated Myths of Dark Muir* by Hugo Bottomly and Florence Fields
- Learn how to get rid of the curse
- Get rid of the curse
- Celebrate with pineapple, ham and olive pizza (Tom's favourite)

It was when we got inside the bookshop that the problems started. For a start there were books *everywhere*. The more we looked, the more books we found. They were piled up on the floor, on tables, under dust sheets. You couldn't move without knocking them over.

"We'll never find the one we need!" I wailed, causing another mini book avalanche.

"My dad used to read me the Harry Potters and there's this bit where Harry, Ron and Hermione have to sneak into the restricted part of the library to find a book. I bet there's a place like that somewhere, where all the really old and dangerous books are," Tom said, weaving past another teetering pile.

We both looked around a bit before Tom pointed to a curtained-off part in the very darkest part of the shop.

"I think I found it," Tom called out as he pulled the curtain back to reveal a wall of old leather books. They were covered in dust and it didn't look like any of them had been touched in years.

"You look through the ones at the top, I'll search the ones at the bottom," Tom said, sliding over the bookcase ladder.

But it's really hard to find what you're looking for when you get your alphabet all mixed up. I started to panic a bit and dropped one of the big heavy books. It crashed to the floor, kicking a dust cloud up around us.

"You don't think we're making too much noise, do you?" I squeaked out through coughs.

"Bit late to worry about that now," Tom coughed back. "Keep looking."

I pulled myself along the shelf until I saw a bright red book. Pulling myself up on to my tiptoes, I reached out for it. I knew as soon as I touched it that it was the right one. It felt hot just like the Serpent's Tooth Rock had the day I made the wish. I pulled it out. And there, shining in gold letters read:

*The Illustrated Myths of Dark Muir*

"I found it!" I called out.

But Tom had gone very still.

"Hey, I said I found it!"

"Shhh," Tom said, as a shadow loomed outside the window.

But there was dust up my nose and I could feel a sneeze coming on. I pressed my hand up against my mouth, but that only made it worse. I could feel the sneeze shaking its way up, until…

"Atchoooooooooo!" It rattled and echoed around the shop.

The shadow moved round to the door and the handle began to wobble.

"Hide!" Tom called out as he flattened himself against a shelf.

But I couldn't hide. I was halfway up a ladder, holding the world's most enormous book. All I could do was freeze.

Mum had once told me that explorer and documentary-maker Osa Helen Leighty said that if you're facing down a bear or a tiger it's best not to move. Just stay perfectly still and try to look big. But I didn't think that was going to work. Mr Sinclair was about to come in, see me stealing a precious antique book, and I was going to be in so much trouble. Da was never going to forgive me. I could hear the rattle of keys. My heart pounded so loudly I was sure Tom could hear it, the man on the other side of the door could hear it, people in Australia could even probably hear it! I thought of how disappointed Mum would be if she was here. I could picture her nose wrinkle, the way it always did just before she got really angry. And then I felt my hand tingle. I dropped the book in shock.

"Hey!" Tom yelled as the book burst open on the floor.

But I wasn't paying attention. Because my hand tingled again. Just like it had the night I'd first disappeared and during the fight with Blair. But this time I didn't want to fight it. I wanted to make it work faster.

I squeezed my hand and mumbled, "I want to disappear…"

My hand grew magically hotter. It was working.

"I want to disappear," I yelled, and this time I could feel my whole body tingle, the magic working faster than ever.

"Amelia, what are you doing?" Tom whispered, his eyes wide.

The bookshop flickered.

"Amelia, stop," Tom said in a tiny panicked voice. "Don't leave me on my own!"

I opened my eyes. Tom's scared face was staring up at me. In my panic I had completely forgotten about him. What was I doing? I couldn't just disappear and leave him. I gripped on to the ladder with all my might, screwed up my eyes and tried to stop. But it was too late, my feet and legs had already vanished. Just as the door flew open, the sound of the ocean poured into my ears and the bookshop faded away.

# Chapter 16

There was the sound of crashing waves and the screech of birds wheeling about in the air. But I convinced myself if I just didn't open my eyes I could still be with Tom. I could still be in the bookshop. In my head I counted to a hundred. I took slow, even breaths. I waited to hear the sound of Tom's voice or to be pulled off the ladder. But the sound of waves was getting louder. And there was another sound: the sound of barking. But not like Pipi's happy bark or even like her excited bark. In fact it wasn't like any dog bark I knew. I opened one eye cautiously and then quickly shut it again.

In the bookshop I had thought the disappearing would take me away from trouble. But I couldn't have been more wrong. I was lying on a beach, on the damp sand. And all around me were the island's herd of big grey seals. And they were not pleased to see me.

Me and Tom had spent hours over the holiday watching the seals from up on the rocks of Seal Beach. I told him how Dark Muir seals were so big because they were really selkies: people who turn into seals in the water. Tom had insisted on naming them all, just like his ponies. But up close they weren't very friendly. They had gathered around me clapping their flippers and rearing up with angry honking barks. The big seal we named Mad Eye, because he was missing one eye, was thumping his way towards me baring his teeth. Mad Eye threw himself up and opened his great mouth and roared. I rolled to the right just as Mad Eye threw himself down next to me. *Thump!* The sand exploded over my face. Mad Eye reared up again. But this time I was on my feet and running as fast as I could, away from the chorus of clapping seals and towards a boat bobbing up and down in the cove.

I jumped into it and pulled the tarp over my head. I lay in the dark waiting for Mad Eye and the other seals to lose interest. A horrible creeping feeling was sneaking up my spine. This gently rocking, red-painted boat was so familiar to me – it wasn't just any boat; this was Mum's. I felt sure the rock's magic had brought me here for a reason. Just like it had taken me to Mum's binoculars, just like it had taken me to her fossil, it had taken me here, to *The Bonny*.

*The Bonny* had been Mum's best surprise. I could remember the day we found it so clearly. It had been after Mum and Da's fights had grown so bad that Mum moved into the attic room. I had thought if I could get Mum out of the attic she would have to make up with Da. I'd done everything: I sprinkled itching powder that I'd bought from the joke shop on Stony Isle on her sheets, I even slipped a big spider under the door. But nothing worked. So I'd sneaked into Da's tool box and stolen his hammer. I was going to break the attic window. There was no way Mum could stay in a room with the rain coming in. But it was impossible to sneak around a house that squeaked under every footstep and Mum had caught me red-handed on the stairs with the hammer. I had thought she'd be so cross, but she wasn't. She didn't even mention it to Da. Instead for the first night in ages she had read to me from *The Little Book of Lady Adventurers*. She'd told me the tale of Anne Bonny, the flame-haired pirate who ruled the Caribbean seas.

Anne Bonny was a fierce young girl who fell in love with a pirate. Turned out of her home by her father, she moved to the famous pirate hideout New

Providence in the Caribbean. There she fell in love with another pirate called Calico Jack Rackham and met Mary Read, a woman who had disguised herself as a man to serve in the navy and then taken to the pirate life. Together they stole a ship and took to the seas to become the scourge of the Caribbean. Anne was so feared in combat that all the pirate crew she served with respected her and she even became a most wanted pirate. After capturing a Spanish ship and hauling in a huge treasure, the king's ship was sent after her. Sadly, after a desperate battle, Anne, Mary and Captain Calico Jack Rackham, along with the rest of the crew, were captured. But Anne managed to escape execution and disappeared – some say to continue her pirate life under a new identity.

I knew the story so well but I loved how Mum added in Anne's own voice, making up things she would say in a very bad Irish accent.

Then the next day Mum had taken me down to Seal Cove where we found a skiff that had washed up. Mum was really excited even though it wasn't much to look at. It was old and a bit rotten and I was pretty sure it had holes in it. But Mum had given me her mischievous look and said, "How about we put that hammer to better use and make a pirate ship?"

Mum and me spent weeks fixing it up. We painted

it red and black just like the picture of Anne Bonny's ship from my book. Mum even found a wooden trunk and fitted it in the keel for holding treasure. And in honour of the pirate queen we named the boat *The Bonny*, painting it in gold letters on the bow. Mum had said it was our magic boat. That it could take us anywhere we wanted to go. And she promised that the next summer we would take it out for real and go on a proper adventure. But Mum didn't come home the next summer, or the one after.

In the end me and Da took *The Bonny* out into the cove. Da made a pirate flag and smashed a beer bottle over the hull for good luck. But sailing *The Bonny* hadn't felt the same without Mum. All I could think about when we were out on the water was all the places in the world she could be.

The pirate flag lay in the bottom of the hull. It looked all sad and crumpled, so I rolled it up and stuck it into the back of my jeans. I'd wished to be with Mum and so far all the disappearing had done was take me to places and to objects – the binoculars, the ammonite, and now the flag – that reminded me of her. I felt like I was starting to piece things together, like I was on the cusp of an adventure. I just wasn't sure what kind of adventure it would be. I desperately needed to talk to Tom about everything.

But with a sharp pain I remembered Tom's poor face in the bookshop.

"Don't leave me," he had said.

But that's just what I had done — left him to face a very angry Mr Sinclair and get in trouble for trespassing. I was very probably the worst friend in the world.

It was already getting dark and Da was expecting me home before dinner. But I couldn't go home without finding out what had happened to Tom. So on my way back I stopped at the bookshop. It was dark again. The closed sign hung on the door and the top window was shut. I pressed my nose against the glass and peered in just to be sure. I couldn't see Tom or the red book I had dropped. In fact, the whole shop looked the same way it had before we broke in. Even the dust covers had been put back over the piles of books. It made me shiver to look at it. It was like nothing ever happened. But I knew it had. I couldn't get Tom's scared face out of my head.

On the way to Tom's farm I kept going over all the ways I would apologize. In my head I came up with thirty-two different ways. I was going to buy Tom every coloured marker I could think of. I was going to clean out pony poo until I was a hundred years old. I even convinced myself I was going to dig out my inflatable flamingo armbands and teach Tom how to swim.

It was pitch black and pouring with rain by the time I sneaked through the pony paddock and up to Tom's grandma's house. I could see Tom in his bedroom, his face lit up in the glow of his computer screen.

"Tom," I called, but he didn't turn around.

I grabbed a stone and threw it up at his window.

"Tom," I yelled again, trying to remember all the important things I had planned to tell him.

He eventually opened the window. His eyes were all puffy and his face looked red. I felt my stomach flip over. I had never seen Tom upset. Not even when he slipped and split his trousers trying to play football. Or when he knocked over a jug of water and ruined his painting in art. Or even when Blair held Colin the fish in the palms of her hands as he thrashed and gasped, until Tom begged her to put him back in his bowl.

"Tom…" I started.

"Go away," he hissed and then slammed the window shut before I could get another word out.

I felt terrible about all the trouble I had got Tom into. I couldn't imagine what his scary grandma was going to do to him. I should have knocked at the door and explained how everything was all my fault. But I didn't. I didn't do anything at all. Instead I ran home. Mum may have named me after two of the most famous lady adventurers, but it looked like I was still the very opposite of brave.

# Chapter 17

It wasn't until I got home that the rain stopped. But this time the black clouds didn't fade away. They hung heavy in the sky, making the occasional thundery crackle. Pipi growled.

*Ar row, row, row,* she barked, spinning herself in circles before coming back to lick me.

I hugged her and breathed in her wet doggy smell.

"I'm all right. Everything's all right," I kept saying, but neither of us believed it.

Pipi whimpered and nibbled at my fingertips.

"Shhh, you'll wake Grandpa."

But I needn't have worried about waking Grandpa up. I could hear him out in the garden and he wasn't alone.

"We found him staring at the cows again," Penny said, stepping into the kitchen.

"Cows, very sinister creatures – always look like they're plotting something. Did you know more people die from cows stampeding than from shark attacks? I was just being vigilant," Grandpa said.

I wasn't in the mood for another of Grandpa's lists of ways he might kick the bucket. And I really didn't want to spend any more time with the terrifying next-door neighbours. I just wanted to crawl into bed and try and forget everything that had happened that day. But I heard Da's jeep rumble up the driveway and I knew I couldn't escape.

"Hello there," Da said in his fake cheery voice. He knew as soon as he saw Hettie and Penny that Grandpa had been making trouble again. I could see his shoulders slump as he walked into the kitchen. So could Grandpa.

"I thought we talked about you not going walkabout on your own," Da said to Grandpa.

"It's not healthy to keep yourself locked inside all day. More people die in their houses than anywhere else, don't you know," Grandpa huffed.

"Thank you for bringing him back," Da said, and paused, expecting Hettie and Penny to say their goodbyes and leave.

"Have you heard about the bookshop? It seems like somebody broke in," Penny said, making herself comfortable on one of the chairs.

"Oh, really?" I said a bit too loudly.

"What on earth could they have wanted?" Da asked, as he dropped a big bag of shopping on to the table.

"Yes, I wonder," Hettie said, and she stared very hard at me. It felt like her gleaming yellow eyes could see right into my head. And not for the first time I thought she knew more about all this strangeness than she was letting on.

"You used to love going there, didn't you, Amelia?" Da said, packing the fridge full of the cheese that made everything smell like feet.

"No. I never go to bookshops. I didn't even know we had a bookshop. I don't even read," I said, overdoing it a bit.

Da shot me the look that said "behave yourself" and I shot him a look right back that said "I am".

"Well, you probably have things to do. I wouldn't want to keep you," Da said to Hettie and Penny, trying not to sound rude. "Thank you for looking out for my da," he added.

But Hettie didn't move or stop staring at me with her intense, golden eyes. "Of course, we must be off to attend to all our important things," she finally said.

"Oh, really?" Penny asked, looking disappointed as Da unpacked the biscuits.

"Yes, things to do, my dear, especially with the storm coming in."

"A storm? I haven't heard anything about it on the shipping news?" Da said.

"Oh, it's going to be a big one," Hettie replied and turned her heavy gaze on me until I thought her amber eyes would drill right into the centre of me.

I didn't realize I was holding my breath until after Hettie and Penny had left. I wondered what they were off to do. Boil up children's bones, eat frogs, or something else equally as terrible. As they pottered down the lane arm-in-arm, Da asked, "You don't know anything about what happened at the bookshop, do you?"

"I wasn't even there," I said, which was half-true. But the thought of disappearing and leaving Tom all alone made me feel bad all over again. I couldn't help it, right then and there at the kitchen table I burst into tears. And it wasn't the kind of crying you could cover up with blowing your nose or pretending you had hay fever. It was the kind of crying that came with embarrassing squeaking noises.

"Hey now, what's this about?" Da said, his eyes filled with worry.

But I didn't know how to answer and I couldn't stop making weird, noisy crying sounds. Pipi nuzzled into me but it didn't make me feel any better.

"What can I do? Is there something you need? Tissues, plasters, a hot drink?" Grandpa asked, looking slightly alarmed.

What I really needed was for Tom not to hate me and for all this truly weird stuff to stop happening. But Da putting his arm around my shoulder helped. I breathed in the musty smell of his wax jacket.

"Did something happen?" Da asked as he stroked my messy hair.

I nodded my head. I wanted to tell him all about the bookshop and Tom and the disappearing. I wanted to tell him everything so badly that it made my insides ache. But even if I could have found the right words, or knew how to explain everything in a way that would make Da believe me, it would just be another case of me causing trouble again. I could already see how disappointed Da would be. So I mumbled something about an argument with Tom and let Pipi lick my toes until I stopped blubbing.

When I had finished wiping my nose on the tea towel Grandpa had passed me, Da decided we all needed cheering up. Grandpa suggested going to the pub, which I thought was quite a good idea. But

Da decided to make the "Da Spectacular" for dinner instead. The "Da Spectacular" is a bit of everything. Eggs, bacon, beans, bubble and squeak, potato smiley faces and, just to be fancy, French toast. It usually takes all of us to make everything. But Grandpa wasn't much help. He kept putting the wrong things in the toaster. Da persuaded him to go and listen to one of his stories on the radio, so we could cook in peace.

But even though everything came out perfectly, I couldn't eat a thing. I couldn't stop thinking about Tom and how angry he had been earlier. So I just pushed my food around my plate and when I thought no one was looking, I fed it to Pipi. Da must have noticed though, because when he came up to my bedroom that night he was carrying a packet of biscuits.

"Just in case you were hungry," he said, "and I thought maybe we might read something. In case you couldn't sleep."

Da used to read to me every night. But I couldn't remember the last time he had done it. So many big things had changed after Mum left that I hadn't noticed all the little things too.

"I'm too old for bedtime stories," I muttered as I tried to disappear under the bedcovers.

"I know," Da said, pulling the cover back and brushing my curly hair out of my face. "But I sort of miss reading our stories, and reading to your grandpa isn't quite the same."

Grandpa only liked to be told grisly ghost stories or whodunnits where everyone got murdered by the butler.

"Well, if you really want to," I said.

Da looked over my bookcase and picked up the lady adventurers book. I'd put it up there to dry after I'd tried to stick it back together. But I hadn't done a very good job. The glue had made the front cover go all wobbly and some of the pages were stuck together.

"What happened to this?" Da asked.

I didn't want to tell him about Blair because then I would have to explain why I had taken the book to school in the first place, so I just shrugged. Da flicked through the sticky pages until he found one Blair hadn't managed to rip out.

"Junko Tabei," Da read, showing me a picture of a small Chinese lady in big sunglasses and orange climbing gear holding a Japanese flag at the top of a snowy mountain.

"Junko Tabei started off as a small and sickly child. But even at a young age she dreamed of scaling mountains. At a time when few women climbed, Junko set her sights on getting to the top of Everest. However, with many people believing women weren't built for climbing, Junko and her team of all-women climbers couldn't find enough money for the trip to Everest. For three years the women trained and fundraised and saved their own money. But it was never enough. Finally, a Japanese newspaper decided to give them the money to get them to the mountain. But a few days into their climb, disaster struck. An avalanche engulfed the camp. With most of the climbers buried under snow, only Junko's guide was left to search for her. He had to dig through a foot of snow only to find most of the climbers injured and Junko unconscious. But despite her close call, Junko was determined to fulfil her dream. Twelve days later she became the first woman to climb Everest."

It was nice having Da read to me. But I couldn't help thinking about Mum and how these were all her stories; she was the intrepid adventurer in the family. Da had never even left Dark Muir. I wished more than anything that I could be with her, far away from this island and my problems.

When Da switched off the light and opened the door I asked, "Do you think Mum will ever come back?"

Sometimes it's easier to ask things in the dark. But either Da didn't hear me, or he pretended not to, because he clicked the door shut behind him.

I couldn't sleep. I kept staring up at my glow-in-the-dark stars and thinking about the book and Tom and everything that was happening with the disappearing. So I pulled out Miss Archibald's blue exercise book from my backpack. I couldn't believe how much I'd written. There were pages and pages of my big blobby handwriting. I'd never written so much in my whole life. But this time I couldn't think where to begin. Every time I had written in my journal before I had imagined talking to Mum and telling her about all the scary mad things that were happening to me. But I wasn't looking forward to telling Mum about how I abandoned Tom. How I hadn't been brave when I needed to be. I closed my eyes and tried to imagine what she might say. How disappointed she would be in me. So I picked up my pen and wrote instead.

Dear Mum,

Here are the things I miss about you:

- I miss how when I had a bad dream you would climb into my bed and we would pretend it was a ship and we were sailing to all kinds of fantastic places until I fell asleep.
- When I really struggled to understand my schoolwork and thought I was stupid, you would take me to Puffin

Cave and we would scream out all the bad thoughts I had and listen to the echoes fade away.

- Most of all I miss you. Because I really need you, Mum. More than ever. Which makes it even harder to keep writing to someone who might never write back.

Before I went back to bed, I pulled out Mum's gold compass from my bedroom drawer. It was still in my birthday box with the ribbon wrapped around it. I tipped it into the palm of my hand and watched the needle wobble. I wished that it would point the way to Mum. But it just twitched and settled on north. Instead of putting it back into the box, though, I pulled the ribbon off and threaded it through the loop at the top. I tied it around my neck. It made me feel better having a little piece of Mum next to my heart.

# chapter 18

After the holidays, everything changed. For a start, Tom wouldn't talk to me at school, and then the weather got worse. A thick mist settled over the island. The days suddenly got darker, the wind was flecked with ice and I could even taste snow in the air. I wore my heavy, yellow rain mac and the red woolly hat and scarf Grandpa had knitted, but I still felt cold and shivery. It was as if everything Hettie and Penny had said was starting to come true.

As the weeks went by, I felt weirder and weirder. My belly was filled with sparkles and my tongue tingled like I had just eaten a giant sherbet dip. And the hand that had touched the Serpent's Tooth Rock felt achy and sore all the time. I was sure something big was going to happen. I just didn't know that everything would start with Miss Archibald's goldfish.

On the first day back after half-term Miss Archibald moved me next to Tom in our STAR class, which would have been awesome if we had been talking. But Tom treated me like I really had disappeared for good. He wouldn't even look at me. Every time I tried to ask him what happened in the bookshop, Tom wouldn't answer. I knew he was upset, because he spent all lesson rearranging his pens in order of colour and height. But he still ignored me. Even Ian and Gregory joined in. Every time I said something they jumped and looked around with a stupid confused look on their faces. Which was really immature, but seemed to make them laugh. I will never understand boys.

Miss Archibald peeped worriedly over her glasses through all of this.

"Has something happened between you and Tom?" she asked after one of our classes.

I hadn't known what to tell her. I watched her rainbow eyebrows crinkle with concern. But I didn't want to get Tom into any more trouble, so I just shook my head.

"You know my door is always open if you need to speak to someone," she said, pushing her glasses back up her beaky nose.

On a list of people I was likely to tell about the disappearing, Miss Archibald was right at the bottom. But I had started to like her. She still looked like an owl but more like a little snowy owl than a stern barn owl. She didn't understand what had happened between me and Tom, and neither did I really. I mean, I knew why Tom was angry. If he had left me to face getting caught all alone, I would be angry too. But I had tried to apologize. I had tried over and over again. I'd even tried to draw Tom a sorry card in art. I had wanted to draw a picture of us on it. But every time I tried to draw Tom, I made him look weird. First I drew him with a big balloon head, and then I accidentally made him look like a giant stick insect, with these long legs that finished off the page. In the end I balled up the card and threw it in the bin. I was about to give up for ever on me and Tom ever being friends again when Blair returned.

Blair had been missing for the whole of the first week back – her mum had taken her on holiday even though that wasn't allowed. I hadn't even noticed she was gone. It's really easy to forget about things like the school bully when your best friend won't talk to you. But Blair certainly hadn't forgotten about me.

When Miss Archibald asked us to pair up for a reading exercise, Blair moved as far away from me as she could. I looked over at Tom desperately but he was already sitting next to Beth, who had spat her hair out in surprise. Gregory was sitting next to Ian obviously. So that just left me and Blair Watson.

"Don't you even think about sitting next to me," Blair growled, but she had gone very pale, ghost pale. Just like she had in science class after I disappeared right in front of her.

I thought of Mum's wildlife advice. "It's best not to look dangerous animals right in the eye." Mum told me that she had learned this from her guide when she was filming wildebeest in Africa. I imagined Blair as a dangerous wildebeest, her pigtails turning into pointy horns in my head. So I edged into the seat next to her, staring straight ahead. But it didn't help. As soon as I was in my seat, Blair thumped the desk.

"Get away from me, freak," she said drawing out the "freak" part.

Blair knew my secret and she wasn't going to keep quiet.

"Look, about what happened when we were fighting. It's not what you think," I stammered, trying to come up with an explanation that didn't involve magical rocks.

But Blair leaned in closer, her dark eyes flashing.

"I know what I saw. You vanished, right in front of

me, because you're a freak with freak powers," she said at the exact moment the class went quiet.

"What was that, Miss Watson?" Miss Archibald asked, looking up from the board.

Every pair of eyes was on Blair. I could tell the whole class had heard what she said, including Tom, who had finally stopped pretending I didn't exist and was staring at me in panic. But the thing was, as soon as Blair said it out loud it sounded just as ridiculous and impossible as when I tried to tell Da for the first time. I looked around. No one believed her. Everyone was whispering and nudging each other.

"Well, Miss Watson, please do share with us," Miss Archibald asked again.

Blair flushed several shades of red and then opened her mouth, but nothing came out.

"Perhaps you can enlighten us after you've finished doing your very best impression of my goldfish," Miss Archibald added, tapping Colin's bowl.

A tiny snigger escaped from me. I tried to cover it up as a cough. I knew making fun of Blair would be the very worst thing I could do. Suddenly I could see Tom in the corner giving me full-force wibbly-wobbly eyebrows that were trying to tell me to stop. But I couldn't help it. After everything that had happened, it felt so good to surrender to the laughter bubbling through my body. My little snigger got louder and louder until it was an unstoppable belly laugh. Then everyone joined in. The whole classroom fell about laughing at Blair Watson.

It took Miss Archibald threatening to make us stay during the break before everyone quieted down. But that didn't stop everyone whispering about it throughout the rest of the lesson. I could even see Gregory do a goldfish impression. Blair saw it too. She twisted in her seat and silently moved a finger across her neck.

"You're dead," she mouthed.

When the break bell went everyone filed out of class still sniggering. As I packed up my things I could see Blair loitering in the library across the hall. She was pretending to read a book but it was upside down and Mr McNevis, our ancient librarian, was nowhere to be seen. I was going to have to plan my escape route very carefully. I ducked behind one of the bookcases when Blair wasn't looking, then peeped around the corner. Tom had come back to grab a folder, which was just the distraction I needed. I crouched down and ran to the bookcase at the end and then darted across to the staircase. I was halfway down the stone steps before I heard Blair shout.

"You better not be sneaking off if you don't want your boyfriend to be in a lot of trouble."

I could have just run, or pretended not to hear. Tom had spent days now being so unfriendly that it would have served him right. But I wasn't going to abandon him. Not again.

In Miss Archibald's classroom Blair was sitting on top of Tom, who was wriggling like an upturned beetle.

"Leave him alone," I said. I was trying to sound brave but my words came out with a wobble.

"Not until I get proof," Blair smirked, then fished her phone out of her pocket and pointed it at me. "If you want your friend back then I want everyone to see what I know I saw you do."

"I can't," I stuttered.

"Oh, we both know you can," Blair said, pushing Tom's head into the carpet. "So show me your freak powers."

"Don't do it, Amelia!" Tom squeaked.

"Oh yeah, and why not?" Blair said pulling at Tom's ear.

"Get off me!" Tom roared, freeing an elbow and shoving it hard into Blair's side. It only knocked Blair back for a second but it was enough for Tom to wiggle his other arm free and pull Blair's long braid. Blair yelped and twisted away, giving Tom enough time to leap to his feet.

"Fine," Blair said, pushing a desk between her and Tom and grabbing my blazer collar, "let's repeat what we did before. I'll punch you and then you do your great vanishing act!"

"Won't be very easy to beat someone up and film it at the same time will it?" Tom said.

"Good point, ostrich boy," Blair snarled as she rushed to the other side of the room and grabbed the fishbowl off Miss Archibald's desk. She gave the bowl a shake, swishing Colin around.

"Fish don't get dizzy," Tom said, brushing himself down and pulling his backpack back on. "Come on, Amelia, let's get out of here."

But I knew Blair wasn't finished. She was smiling that same terrible smile she had on her face the day she destroyed my precious book.

"You know what else fish don't do?" Blair said, smirking as she stepped over to the open window. "Fly!" she finished, balancing Colin's bowl precariously on to the window ledge.

Tom rushed forward.

"No, no, no." Blair said, one hand rocking the fish bowl. "You don't want to make my hand slip."

Tom took a step back and I could see he had his fists clenched so tight that his knuckles had turned white.

"Now see, I can easily hold this goldfish bowl in one

hand and film with the other. So either you're going to reveal to the world what a massive freak you are, or Colin is going to have a very unfortunate accident," she said, her lip curling into a cruel little grin.

I knew Blair was mad, but she wasn't a fish killer, was she?

"Y-you wouldn't," I stammered.

Blair narrowed her eyes and wobbled the bowl closer to the edge.

"You wanna bet?" she said.

I looked at Colin helplessly sloshing around in his bowl and then at Tom's poor frightened face. And I thought about how I had disappeared for all the wrong reasons in the bookshop. If I did it now, no matter how much trouble it got me into, it would be for the right ones.

I closed my eyes and whispered, "I want to disappear."

"Amelia, don't," Tom called out.

But my mind was made up.

"I want to disappear," I said louder and clenched my right hand into a tight fist, expecting at any moment for my hand to grow hot, the room to wobble and my secret to be out for ever. But nothing happened.

"How long is this supposed to take?" Blair sighed, waving the flash of her camera phone's light on me.

I closed my eyes and yelled, "I want to disappear," just like I had in the bookshop.

But something wasn't working. No matter how hard I clenched my fist, I couldn't get my hand to grow hot. Then I felt Tom's hand in mine.

"Amelia, stop," he said and I opened my eyes.

I was still standing in the tiny classroom that smelled of board markers and Miss Archibald's fruity perfume, with the sound of the rain belting against the windows and Blair Watson holding a fish to ransom.

"I can't do it," I said and this time I wasn't lying.

My hand wasn't even a little bit hot; it wasn't tingling. I didn't know how I'd managed to make the disappearing work in the bookshop. But I hadn't been able to do it again.

"YES YOU CAN!" Blair shouted. "I know what I saw. So no matter what, I promise you I'm going to prove it. One way or another," she finished, giving me a look that made my insides turn to jelly.

And then she tipped Colin out of the window.

## Chapter 19

It didn't take long for Miss Archibald to notice Colin was missing. Every time she looked over at the empty bowl she sniffed and wrinkled her beaky nose like she was holding back tears. But she wouldn't move the bowl off her desk. I think she believed it would make the culprit come forward out of guilt. But I knew that was never going to happen. If anything, Blair had become even more awful. It made me wish that I could tell Miss Archibald what had happened. But Tom and I were in enough trouble already without telling on Blair. So Colin's disappearance was just another secret I was going to have to keep.

There were so many secrets, that I had to make a list to keep track of them.

**Amelia's Secrets**

- I can disappear. (That's kind of the biggest one.)
- I broke into a bookshop.
- I know who killed Miss Archibald's fish.
- Blair Watson is out to get me.

I hadn't been the only one keeping secrets. Tom had too. I could tell he was bursting to spill them to me. But Miss Archibald wouldn't stop babbling on about the end of term assembly, even though it was months away.

"Right," she announced. "I know some of you have made great progress with your reading skills so it's time I revealed that one member of our class is going to get the very special honour of reading out an essay based on their journal project in the end of year assembly." She paused, waiting for us to react.

The room was silent.

"OK, it's optional. No one has to do it, if they don't want to. But I think we've all been making so much progress in our lessons that it would be really wonderful for our class to be represented in this year's assembly," Miss Archibald continued. "And readers at the assembly will be up for a prize of a trip to the local owl sanctuary!"

You could have heard crickets chirp.

"And a ten pound book voucher."

You could have heard baby crickets chirp.

Miss Archibald sighed.

"Also, to prepare for the assembly you will be excused from summer sports day, including the cross-country run."

There was a ripple of approval from the class and Gregory and Ian rushed up to stick their names in the empty fishbowl.

"I'm going to leave this out until the end of term. Just in case anyone else is a bit shy about putting their name forward," Miss Archibald said, eyeing the rest of the class from over the top of her glasses.

Miss Archibald was delusional if she thought I was going to get up and read in front of hundreds of people. I could see myself stuttering and mumbling through the whole first page and everyone laughing. Just thinking about it made me feel like a bowling ball was sitting in the pit of my stomach. I could see Tom staring over at me from his table at the front. He didn't look tempted either. He stuck his tongue out at me. Ever since the fish incident we had gone back to being friends, but between Tom being grounded over the weekend and all my schoolwork, neither of us had had a proper opportunity to talk. It wasn't until Monday break that I got the chance. As soon as I saw

Tom coming out of STAR class I pulled him into the girls' loo.

"We have to stop hanging out in here," Tom said nervously, looking under the stalls to check if we were alone.

"I've been trying to talk to you ever since what happened with Blair."

"Me too. But I've been grounded and I'm not allowed to use the phone, or the computer. I'm not even meant to be hanging around with you. My parents think you're a bad influence because I've never been in trouble before, not until we became friends."

"I'm so sorry, Tom," I said, staring down at my shoes. "If I could take it all back I would."

"I know, I found your card," Tom said, pulling out the strange bubble-headed drawing I thought I had thrown away in art class. "You don't really think I look like that, do you?"

I grinned.

"Only if you think I look like *that*," I said, pointing to the crazy scribble-haired drawing of me next to the one of him. "So you got caught?"

"Yeah, about a second after you disappeared, Mr Sinclair found me."

"Did he call the police?"

Tom shook his head.

"Worse. He called my gran."

I sucked the air in through my teeth, imagining the scary little lady I had seen at Tom's door.

"She made me clean up the whole shop without saying a word and then when I got home I had to tell my parents and they didn't say anything for the longest time. We just sat and ate dinner with Mum looking like she might cry until finally Dad said he was really disappointed in me," Tom said.

I scrunched up my face. "Sorry," I said again, because I knew "disappointed" was pretty much the worst thing an adult can say to you. Worse than getting mad, or even yelling at you. It meant they didn't trust you any more.

"Then Gran went and banned me from looking after the ponies for a bit. And she said if I so much as forgot a pencil at school, let alone got into any more trouble, she would sell them off so she could focus on teaching me manners," Tom continued.

I felt bad all over again. If there was one thing Tom loved more than anything on the planet, it was his ponies.

"So why are you helping me?" I asked.

"Because I'm still your friend, stupid, even when I'm mad at you."

That was one of the best things about Tom; he had

a way of making even the most complicated things sound simple.

"And I guess we're even now. You coming back to save me from Blair. But, Amelia, what were you thinking trying to disappear in front of her? Can you imagine what she'd do with a video of that? Can you imagine what would happen to you?" Tom said shaking his head.

But that was the thing. I didn't know what was happening to me! I knew I could disappear and when I did it took me to places and objects that were important to Mum and me. But I didn't know why and I didn't know how to stop it. There was so much I didn't understand.

"I wish we'd been able to get that book because I need to know what's happening to me," I said.

Tom smiled. "I think it's time I showed you that Operation Bookshop wasn't a complete disaster," he said, pulling out a folder from his backpack. "Just before I got caught I managed to shove some of the pages of the book that came loose down my trousers."

I couldn't help but gasp as Tom showed me the pages. They were filled with swirly inky drawings, full of dark forests and glittery stars. The kind of pictures that should have big, gold dragons and silvery princesses in midnight blue castles in them. But instead they were drawings full of the places I knew from around the island. I had only ever thought of Dark Muir as a cold island in the middle of nowhere. But these pictures made it feel magical.

"This section is about the rock," Tom said, his eyes shining.

Tom handed me a page. *The Myth of Serpent's Tooth Rock* it read, and underneath was a picture of the rock rising above a black–and–blue sea.

"Do you really think this is going to explain what's happening to me?"

"I think so," Tom said,

My hands trembled as I turned over the page. A giant snake's head leered out at me. Its golden eyes looked almost real and its scales glittered in silvery ink. I blinked trying to read the swirly writing.

"Do you want me to read it?" Tom asked and I nodded. He turned to a page with a picture of a starry night overlooking a glittery snake twisting its way through giant waves.

"*In the beginning there were no islands. Only sea as far as you could see. Until one day the serpent of the world awoke. With a flick of his great tail, the seas parted and an island sprung up. With a wobble of his body another island sprung up and, with one great toss of his head, Dark Muir appeared from the waters. The snake yawned; he was so tired after creating all the islands that he fell asleep, letting only one tooth poke above the water,"* Tom read.

"I know this story. It's the one Grandpa used to tell me."

"There's more," Tom said, bouncing up and down. Shakily, I watched as Tom turned over the page. All the stars from the previous page had been replaced by snow. And the island was engulfed in inky black clouds and silvery lightning.

*"Over time the angry sea and roaring wind tried to claim back the islands. But no matter how hard the wind blew or how high the waves grew, they could never harm Dark Muir, because it was protected by the magic of the serpent's tooth,"* Tom read, turning to a page with a picture of the snake wrapping itself around Dark Muir. Its glittery head resting on the cliff tops, its tail cradling Sometimes Island, casting a golden ring of protection.

*"But once in a while the serpent grows tired of watching the island and chooses to transfer its power temporarily by granting a wish. That's why every year when an islander turns eleven they set out to make a wish. If chosen, the serpent gives that person a power to fulfil their wildest dreams. A power that grows stronger and stronger until the wish finally comes true."* Tom's eyes were growing wider and wider.

*"However, without the protection of the serpent's magic the angry sea and jealous wind will try to take back the island."* I gasped as he turned to a picture of Dark Muir being engulfed by gigantic waves.

*"Only the return of the wish can grant the islands safety once more,"* Tom finished, putting the pages down shakily.

"Amelia," he whispered. "What did you wish for?"

But before I could answer the bell went.

# Chapter 20

I had thought the book would explain everything that was happening to me, but it just created more questions.

- Would the disappearings eventually take me from places that meant something to Mum, to Actual Mum herself?
- Was the island really in danger from a terrible storm?

Thinking about it all made my head spin. I needed to tell Tom everything as soon as possible after school. But I had to get through the day without running into Blair first, and she hadn't been lying when she said she would stop at nothing to expose my secret.

After the fish incident Blair had rallied her ponytail gang to spread the word that I was public enemy number one; that I had weird freaky powers and for the good of the school I needed to be exposed. And even though nobody really believed Blair's story about me disappearing, it was much better to be Blair Watson's friend than her enemy. Especially as Gregory and Ian had been found locked in a store cupboard in nothing but their PE shorts after they'd played a prank on her. So it soon became apparent that it was the whole year's mission to catch me doing something weird. Blair's spies were everywhere that day. Waiting for me in the girl's loos, stalking me on the field, sitting too close to me in assembly. Even our special lunchtime spot under the stage wasn't safe. Me and Tom couldn't walk around a corner without someone pointing a camera phone at us. I had gone from the strange home-schooled girl who nobody talked to, to the most famous girl in school!

When I had started school, I had dreamed about being popular, about having a big group of friends who I could invite around my house, sharing secrets and having sleepovers. I'd never really minded not having many friends when Mum had been about. We didn't need anyone else to make our adventures any better. But after she left I'd watched everyone in their friendship groups in church or at the cinema and I'd longed with every bit of me to be part of one. To not be the loneliest girl on the island. But Blair had made it so I couldn't even go to the loo on my own. I kept waiting for it to calm down, but more and more kids joined in. Half of them didn't even know Blair or about my supposed disappearing powers. It had just become the popular thing to do. It made it impossible for me and Tom to have a top-secret meeting.

It was a few days later when Tom managed to sneak me a note during STAR class. It had a funny picture of me and Tom on the front dressed like ninjas complete with swords.

"At break meet me back at the library. Take the long way around. Don't be followed."

It was the not-getting-followed instruction that turned out to be the hardest bit. Even though Tom and I split up, Blair was tracking me almost as soon as I got into the corridor. She was joined by the redheaded twins as soon as we were down the stone steps. I knew they wouldn't come too close as some of the teachers had started to cotton on to what was going on. She knew how to tail me whilst acting like she was doing something perfectly innocent like looking at posters or listening to music with her friends. Blair might have been mad but she wasn't stupid. I was wondering how

I was ever going to lose them when Miss Archibald poked her head out of her office on the first floor corridor.

"Ah, Amelia, just who I was looking for," Miss Archibald said, ushering me into her office.

I saw Blair and the rest of the ponytail gang glower as Miss Archibald shut the door.

"Amelia, I've been really impressed by some of the work you've been doing in class. But I think you might benefit from using some extra tools, something to help make reading a bit easier. I've got some coloured sheets I think you should try," Miss Archibald said, faffing around in her desk drawer. "I must have left them in the classroom. I'll be right back."

As Miss Archibald opened the door I could see Blair and the ponytail gang still lurking in the corridor. Chloe looked more miserable than ever. I let the door slam shut and looked around desperately for an escape. There was a narrow window over Miss Archibald's desk. I climbed up and wiggled the rusted latch free. I squeezed my head and elbows out, then my right leg, but my bum got a bit stuck and my horrible itchy skirt got caught on the latch. I could hear footsteps coming back up the corridor. I didn't know what was worse: being followed by Blair, or getting caught halfway out a window by Miss Archibald. So I took a deep breath and started wriggling. Bit by bit, parts of me started to come free, and with an awful rip I was on the other side of the window.

It wasn't too hard to sneak back into the building. Blair and her cronies had already gone off to look for me elsewhere. And the corridor was empty otherwise.

Tom was already waiting for me in the library, looking red, sweaty and covered in something gooey.

"I swear I nearly didn't make it. A whole group of year seven girls started following me, so I had to hide in a wheelie bin. And trust me, they are much harder to get out of than to get into," he panted.

I grinned and picked an old straw from Tom's bristly hair.

"So what's the plan?" I asked.

"Follow me," Tom said as he led me down the stone staircase and yanked me through an old hinged door with a sign reading Out of Bounds. I had walked past this door so many times, but I'd never even wondered what was behind it.

Tom slipped his metal ruler out of his bag. And, pushing it into the crack in the door where the lock was, he wiggled it until I heard the lock go click.

"I told you I had everything in the bag!" Tom grinned.

As soon as my eyes adjusted to the dark, I gasped. If this had been a fairy tale then this would have been the room at the top of the castle that they locked the princess in. The only light came through narrow slit windows, the kind that archers might have used to fire on enemies below. And the whole room was filled floor to ceiling with tables and chairs and even a dusty old piano, all covered in glittering spiderwebs.

"Where are we?" I asked.

"Gregory and Ian showed me this place when they figured out the lock trick. Apparently it used to be where they kept the weapons when this was a real castle. When Bridlebaine first opened, this was the music room, until the piano fell through the floor and crushed the head girl. Apparently."

"Should we be in here?" I asked as the floorboards gave a loud groan.

"Don't worry. It's fine as long as you don't jump up and down," Tom said, clearing the dust off a piano seat and setting up a fold-out chair for me.

"So," he said, when we were both settled. "I think it's time you told me the whole story."

I started before I'd even made the wish. I started right at the beginning on the day Mum left.

Tom sat in silence for a very long time. I could tell he was bursting to jump in with questions. But he didn't. He let me tell him about how Mum and Da hadn't stopped arguing, how Mum had moved into the attic room and how nothing I could do would make her move back. He let me tell him about how one day out of the blue she announced she had a new filming job. How I had tried to stop her going. But after our camping trip she had made up her mind. How it had been nearly two years since she had left.

Eventually Tom said, "And you don't think she's going to come back?"

I shook my head. I couldn't tell Tom the awful part. The reason why.

"And you don't know where she is?" Tom said.

I shook my head again. I didn't have a clue where she was. The closest I had been to finding her, to being with her, was when the rock's magic had taken me to places that brought special memories of my mum to the surface. But the pages Tom had taken from the shop spoke of this magic growing stronger, to the point that the wish was fulfilled. Which means it could take me to Mum. This made me very much not want it to stop happening.

"Amelia, let me help you find your mum. My dad used to be a policeman; he said there's loads of ways to track people down. He cracked a burglary ring by bidding for a thirty-foot stolen panda on eBay. He says there's hundreds of ways to find people just on the internet. You just have to know how to look for them."

I chewed my lip. I wasn't completely convinced by Tom's plan.

"But if the disappearing is really going to take me to Mum…" I started.

"But what if it doesn't. What if it goes wrong? What if something terrible happens? What if a storm destroys Dark Muir like that book warns?"

I thought of how scared I had been trapped in the bog, that first time I'd disappeared. How I nearly hadn't made it home.

"That wish, the transfer of power, it's dangerous, Amelia. Didn't you see how everyone was scared when the rock disappeared?"

I bit my lip and thought of what Grandpa had said: "The rock grants wishes at a terrible price." My stomach churned as I looked at the inky storm on the pages in front of me.

"You need to transfer the power back to the rock – then the island will be protected again," Tom said.

"But we don't know how," I said.

"I bet it's in that book. We just have to get the rest of the pages. But Amelia you have to promise me you won't use your powers to disappear again. It brings the storm closer when you do."

"I don't even know if I can control what's happening to me. I tried when Blair threatened us, but nothing happened."

"That's probably a good thing. Can you imagine what she would have done if she'd got a recording of that?"

The thought made me shiver.

"So we're agreed. You're not to use your powers again?"

I nodded.

"Promise?" Tom asked, offering me his pinkie finger.

I was still scared of the disappearing and the dark, inky storm illustrations in the book, so I wanted to agree with everything Tom had said. But as we linked pinkie fingers I knew in my heart that I wouldn't be able to keep my promise. Because if there was no more magic, there would be no chance of finding Mum.

# Chapter 21

It didn't take long for me and Tom to perfect our ninja-style escapes to the room under the castle stairs. All we had to do was split up after a lesson had finished, find a good hiding place and, when the coast was clear, head for the library. There were more hiding places in Bridlebaine Academy then you could imagine! And Tom and I had found them all. We had hidden in supply cupboards, trees and even in the recycle bin once. Although after I got covered in cobwebs and sticky yoghurt pots, I decided that bins were to be avoided. But we had become so good at hiding that eventually most of our year got bored trying to follow us. This made Blair Watson furious, because on her own she was no match for our ninja skills. Or so we thought.

Over December the tower room had grown so cold that we had to build an igloo out of broken fold-up chairs and dust blankets. But even in our igloo, with our hats and gloves on, our teeth wouldn't stop chattering.

"What have you found out?" I asked Tom.

"Not much, but next weekend is the last one I'm grounded for. Then I can use the computer and we can do a proper search for your mum," Tom said.

"What about getting hold of the rest of the book?" I asked.

"I thought about that too," Tom said. "I thought I could ask Mr Sinclair if I could help out at the shop for free, to say sorry. If Gran thinks I've taken my punishment seriously and am really trying to make amends I'm sure she'd convince Mr Sinclair to take me on."

Suddenly there was a loud screech and a burst of light. The door to the tower room had been flung open. Tom put a finger over his mouth and peeped out under the dust cover.

"Blair," he mouthed silently to me and I could feel my heart jump.

"Come out, come out, wherever you are," Blair sang, the heels of her pointy black boots thumping on the creaky old floorboards.

"Where could they be?" Blair asked no one in particular as she upturned an old table, making the whole room shudder.

Tom was trying to communicate a complicated escape plan in sign language but I felt frozen to the spot.

"If you know what's good for you, you'll come out. I know you're up here..." Blair said as she kicked the piano stool across the room. It flew into a pile of chairs with a sickening *bang*.

"Run," Tom said, grabbing my hand as an avalanche of chairs swept across the floor.

But Blair reached the door before us.

"I knew you were hiding around here!" she yelled triumphantly.

"What are you doing?" Tom bellowed. "You could have got us all crushed!"

But Blair wasn't listening. She was staring at me.

"What is that?" Blair said, with a glint in her eyes.

I looked down. In all the running my mum's compass had slipped out of my shirt.

"That's how you do it, isn't it?" Blair shouted. "You've got some kind of magic necklace."

"N-no," I stuttered, desperately trying to tuck it back under my shirt collar. "It's just a necklace."

"Oh, yeah? Well you won't mind letting me have a look at it, then."

I tried to back away but I tripped over one of the fallen chairs and into the piano. It gave a tuneless tinkle as Blair ripped the ribbon from around my neck.

"Give it back," Tom said, trying to grab for it.

"Or what?" Blair snarled, pushing Tom out of the way as she strode over to the window.

"So how does it work, then?" she asked, holding the compass up and letting it twist in the light. I could see my mum's initials glimmer.

"I told you: it doesn't. It's just a compass, all right? It used to belong to my mum," I said, the word "mum" getting stuck in my throat.

I knew if Mum were here, she would have refused to let me be scared of Blair Watson. She would have told me that if Amelia Earhart had been scared, she wouldn't have been the first woman to fly across the Atlantic Ocean. But I couldn't help myself. No matter how hard I bit my lip, I couldn't stop the tears welling up.

"I'm going to get a teacher!" Tom yelled as he stumbled over the chairs and out the door.

But Blair didn't seem to care. She was rubbing the compass like it was a magic lamp.

"I want to disappear," she whispered.

But of course nothing happened.

"How do you make it work?" Blair said, shaking it.

"It's just an old compass," I said, sniffing back tears.

Blair shook it again and put it up to her ear. Then she turned it over in her hand while muttering.

"You're right, it's just a dumb old compass," she sighed.

She held the compass out to me but just as I went to grab it she snatched it back.

"No use to me then, is it?" she hissed. And I watched her arm wind back in what felt like slow motion.

"Stop!" I half-managed to get out before she threw the compass across the room.

I could hear the crack as it hit the stone wall. When I turned to look I could see bits of shattered glass shining up from the floor and a big ugly dent in the gold case. I ran over and picked it up, cradling it in my hands. It was broken: the compass needle no longer pointed north; it could no longer always point me in the right direction home. I roared and threw myself at Blair, who stumbled on the pile of chairs and went crashing to the ground just as the door flew open.

"Amelia Hester McLeod!" Miss Archibald bellowed.

It was the first time I'd heard my full name at Bridlebaine Academy. So I knew I was in big trouble.

"It's not what it looks like," Tom squeaked as I realized I was on top of Blair, her horrid ponytail in my hand ready to be pulled hard.

"Well, it looks like Amelia was halfway to strangling Blair with her own hair," Miss Archibald said, raising an eyebrow in the most dramatic fashion.

"Blair started it. Amelia was just trying to defend herself," Tom protested.

"So you were up here too, in the out-of-bounds room when this happened?" Miss Archibald asked, her eyebrow arching so far up I was afraid it was going to fly off her face.

"You could have had a serious accident up here," she continued sternly. "I'm sorry, Tom, but I'm going to have to inform your parents about this."

Tom turned white. He had only just worked off being grounded the first time. His parents and his grandma were going to be furious. I tried to squeeze his hand but he shuffled away.

"No, don't! I mean there's no need. Because I was never in the out-of-bounds room!"

Miss Archibald pushed her round glasses up her nose. "I see. So how did you know to come and get me?"

"It's just; I went to the library to get this book. This book on, um, football."

Miss Archibald narrowed her eyes over her glasses.

Tom was literally the least sporty kind of person there could be. Watching Tom try to play football was like watching a spider try to tap dance.

"So I was reading my book about football. Because I love football, obviously. So I was up there, in the library, reading all the fascinating things about the kicking of balls into nets. When I heard a sound and then some crashing and then, well, I came and got you."

I couldn't believe it. Tom was lying! And he wasn't even doing a good job of it.

Miss Archibald sighed heavily.

"So if I have all this right, you were busy educating yourself on the joys of the beautiful game when you heard a fight and thinking only of doing the right thing you ran to inform me?"

Tom nodded, avoiding my eye.

"Well, in that case you couldn't have possibly seen who started the fight?"

"No, miss," Tom said, looking down at his feet.

Miss Archibald folded her arms and made a face like she had just sucked on a very sour lemon.

"Well, then, I can only go on what I saw which is that you were both very much involved in this fight," Miss Archibald said, looking at Blair's pulled out ponytail and my ripped collar. Then she shook her head.

"I would expect this kind of behaviour from Miss

Watson, but from you, Amelia? I thought we were making progress. I know you had some problems settling in here, but I've seen how well you're doing in geography and how bright some of your answers are. And I thought after our little chat you might finally find your feet. But maybe a school setting isn't right for you after all. Maybe I need to have a serious chat with your da."

I opened my mouth but no words would come out. It was like they were all scrambled up in my head. I looked at Tom desperately, but he just kept staring at his feet. I couldn't believe he was going to let me take the blame. It was his idea to come up here and it was Blair who had broken my compass. I could feel the shards of glass digging into my palm. I wanted so badly for Tom to speak up and explain the truth and make Miss Archibald, the one teacher I liked, understand. But Tom turned away and Miss Archibald just carried on shaking her head. And what was even worse was Blair smiled through everything. She didn't care that she was in trouble. She was always in trouble! Her parents probably don't even notice any more. Her da wasn't going to be disappointed and her mum wasn't going to leave like mine did.

"Fighting in this school is unacceptable. There are

going to be some very serious consequences," Miss Archibald said as she began to list them.

But I couldn't listen any more and I couldn't look at Blair's smug face. Or Tom's lying one. Out of everyone I knew, I trusted Tom the most: he knew all my secrets, and I didn't share those with anyone. I had even told him about my mum. Tom letting me down was worse than any punishment Miss Archibald could give me. It was even worse than Mum's compass being broken. My hand squeezed the compass as I thought how much I wanted to be with Mum, far away from this room, this school, these islands. And that's when I felt my hand tingle.

This wasn't like any of the other times, the times when I had been afraid of the magic making me disappear or when I had harnessed it out of desperation. With the compass in my hand I could feel the pull of the rock's magic. I could feel it wanting to help me find Mum. And I didn't want to fight it any more.

"So the first thing that will happen is an official report of the incident will be sent to your parents," Miss Archibald carried on.

But I didn't wait to hear the second thing. I squeezed the compass and bolted down the stone steps and into the first-floor corridor. I heard Miss Archibald yell and Tom shout "Amelia!" in a scared little voice.

But I didn't care about either of them. I didn't care about the extra trouble I was getting myself into or that I was about to break my promise to Tom. I only cared about one thing.

As I sprinted down the stairs, I thought of all the times Mum had read me stories of brave explorers and all the times we visited Puffin Cave together and all the times she made me laugh so hard when she made up the completely wrong words to a song on the radio. I felt the compass in my hands grow hotter. I could hear Miss Archibald's heels clacking after me and Tom's voice bouncing around the empty corridor. But I didn't open my eyes. I squeezed my hand, felt it get hot.

"I want to disappear," I murmured.

The sound of the ocean poured into my ears as my eyes snapped open. The corridor flickered as Miss Archibald, Blair and Tom appeared breathlessly from around the corner.

"I want to disappear," I whispered again and my legs vanished.

"I told you!" Blair shouted triumphantly.

Miss Archibald ripped off her glasses, her mouth a perfect round O of horror. Blair grabbed for her phone. But before she could pull it out, the bell went. Children poured into the corridor, knocking Miss Archibald's glasses out of her hands and pushing Blair back. In the middle of the crowd I could see Tom towering over everyone. He was waving his arms desperately for me to stop. But it was too late. With the crackle of thunder, we both knew what was going to happen next.

# Chapter 22

If I was to write a list of All Time Stupid Things to Absolutely Never Do, at the top of that list would be:

DISAPPEARING FROM SCHOOL

It didn't take long for me to regret what happened. I'd disappeared in front of so many witnesses, one of them being the only teacher I liked. I was going to be in so much trouble when I went back. But that wasn't the biggest reason why I was terrified of what I had done.

Which brings me to number two on my All Time Stupid Things to Absolutely Never Do list.

DISAPPEARING AT SCHOOL WITHOUT A PLAN

Mum always said that the best explorers have plans. Just like Ida Reyer Pfeiffer, who before going to visit a tribe of cannibals learned how to say in their language, "I am too old and tough so would not be good to eat." It saved her life. But back in the corridor I hadn't had a plan. I hadn't really been thinking at all.

I opened my eyes, blinking into the dark. I could hear birds but I knew I wasn't on Sometimes Island. I could hear the sea too, but I knew this wasn't Seal Beach. And I knew this definitely wasn't the boys' loos. My eyes adjusted to the dark and I didn't have to wonder where I was any more. The magic had disappeared me and brought me back to the place where everything had begun. It had brought me to Puffin Cave.

The light cast rainbows across the cave walls and the sound of the sea rushed and whooshed around me. I struggled up. The cave floor was covered in rough rocks, but beside me was one so shiny it shone like a diamond. I picked it up and rolled it in my hand; it was just a piece of glass polished by the sand and sea. But Mum had always thought finding these were special.

"It's not quite a fossil, Amelia, but it takes hundreds of tides to make this. And that makes it something worth having." She had said this every time we found one in the cave.

I had found loads of them because Puffin Cave had always been mine and Mum's special place. It was where she took me whenever I felt upset.

"Just yell out all the things you're sad about," she used to say.

And we would fill up the cave with all our bad thoughts, hear them ricochet and echo off the walls and then listen to them fade away. And as they faded, some of their pain and power faded too. This place had always made me feel better. Right up until I had done the awful thing.

It was a few days before my tenth birthday. Back when Mum still telephoned sometimes. Back when I thought she might come back to me.

I asked the question I had asked a million times.

"When are you coming home?"

I could hear Mum sigh all the way from Australia where she was filming a documentary about kangaroos.

"Not for a little bit, Amelia," Mum had said. "But I was thinking if I get some time off from filming that I could come and visit for your birthday."

I had been so excited until Mum had said the next bit.

"And maybe it would be all right if I brought a friend…?"

I tried to think of all the friends of Mum's that

I knew. There was Miss Wilson from the sweet shop and Tony, the guy Da hired to help out on the boat sometimes. And there were the Selkie Swimmers who Mum would sometimes join for an ice-cold dip. But If I really thought about it, Mum didn't have any proper friends on Dark Muir.

"Who's the friend?" I asked, confused.

"Bob from work. He's a producer on the documentary I'm making." Then Mum's voice went all strange. "He's a very special friend, Amelia. I'd like you to get to know him."

But I didn't want to get to know Bob. I knew if Mum came home with him that she and Da would never get back together. And then she would leave me forever.

"I don't think so. Me and Da have planned all these special things for just the two of us," I lied.

"Oh," Mum said, her voice all sad and small. "Well, I don't want to come back and get in the way of anything."

"Then you shouldn't have left in the first place!" I yelled and once the words tumbled out of my mouth I felt a wave of anger crash over my body. "Da's right: we're much better off without you," I added meanly.

The phone line went quiet. I could hear Mum sob

softly but I was too angry to take back what I'd said. I just let the words hang in the air and listened to the crackles on the phone line.

"Amelia," Mum finally said, her voice all strangled.

But I didn't want to hear anything else. Because it wasn't like talking to my mum any more, it was like talking to a stranger, a stranger who had friends called Bob and never came home. So I hung up.

Mum didn't come home for my tenth birthday, but I knew she would still give me a special phone call. I couldn't face it, not after the last one, so I ran away. There had only been one place to run and hide on Dark Muir and that was Puffin Cave. When Da finally found me I had lost my voice yelling into the cave and filled my pockets full of bits of sea glass. I thought he would be so angry at me for running away, but he wasn't. He helped me wash the sea glass clean in the waves and then wrapped his big arms around me. We sat there for a very long time listening to the water until it got dark and I felt ready to talk about what had happened. Afterwards, Da had shown me the seven stars that made up the Big Dipper and together we found the big, bright North Star. That night Da stuck the plastic stars on my ceiling and we made up our own constellations. It had been one of the worst and best birthdays rolled into one.

Outside, I could hear the screeching of puffins and the roar of the ocean. And the roar was getting louder. Water trickled in around me. I struggled up to my feet. My legs still felt wobbly, but I didn't have time to lie around. I could hear the crash and froth of the waves outside of the cave. The tide was coming in and soon Puffin Cave would be completely underwater. I could feel a shiver run up my spine that had nothing to do with the cold. Shakily, I got to my feet.

"I want to disappear," I said. Waiting for my hand to grow warm and the cave to flicker.

But nothing happened.

I squeezed my fists, held my breath and closed my eyes.

"I want to disappear," I said again, but the words felt all wrong just like they had in Miss Archibald's classroom with Blair. They simply wouldn't work.

The water in the cave was rushing in faster.

"Hellllpppppp!" I roared, and my panic boomed around the cave.

But no one could hear me. No one even knew where I was. Not Miss Archibald, not Tom, not even Da. I was going to have to escape myself.

The only way out was to climb the cliffs. Up above the sea caves were the old cliff steps, but they were steep and slippery and mostly worn away. Mum had always used a rope and harness when she went to check on the puffin nests.

Outside the cave, I pulled myself up along the rocky edge and hauled myself over the rocks. The sea crashed around me, the wind whipped my knotty hair against my face and my eyes stung with the cold. The weather had changed again, just like it had the other times I disappeared. But it wasn't the inky storm from the book. Or the rumbly thunderstorms from earlier. From the dazzling white sky, snowflakes fell as soft and light as feathers. They vanished as quickly as they hit my skin, leaving me shivering as I edged out of the cave and on to the dangerous steps. I pulled my school blazer tight around me and thought of Tom and Blair. They would probably be in science now, listening to Mr McNair and his daft jokes. I'd never wanted to be in a lesson so badly.

The puffins whirled and groaned above me, as I edged my foot on to a broken step. It was slick with seaweed. Carefully, I edged my way up the first few. Then the wind caught me and threw me back. I slipped against the sharp rock face, grazing my arm and bashing my elbow. I hugged the wall and watched as bits of loose rock tumbled past.

*Just think good thoughts, think good thoughts,* I said to myself over and over in my head. But I couldn't help but do a Grandpa and think of all the terrible ways I could die:

- Drowning
- Falling
- Being eaten by puffins

I closed my eyes and tried to think of one of Mum's explorer stories; they always calmed me down. I thought of the story of Junko Tabei, who had survived being buried by an avalanche to become the first woman to climb Everest. I could picture Junko in her orange climbing suit waving a Japanese flag from the top of the mountain. I looked up at Puffin Cliffs and tried to picture myself at the top waving a Scottish flag. The first girl to scale the cliffs of Dark Muir. I screwed up all my courage, grabbed the old guard rail with both hands and hauled myself up on to the slippery staircase. Below me I heard the wild whoosh of the waves. I gripped the cold metal rail again and climbed higher, but the wind buffeted me back and my hands slipped. My legs slid out from beneath me. I managed to catch on to the bottom of the rail before I tumbled off. But I was dangling on the edge, my legs swaying in the wind. Snow swirled around me. The only thing stopping me from falling into the sea was my grip on the rest of the rail. But then it creaked.

The rail started to pull away from the edge. I swung my knee up on to the nearest step, but I missed. I swung again and the rail shuddered and groaned.

"One more time," I whispered.

With one last effort my leg hooked on to the step. I pulled myself back up on to the carved stairway, just as the guide rail came away. With a huge splash, it plummeted into the rising sea.

The puffins circled above me, making their chirping cries. But I couldn't move. I felt glued to the edge. One step more and I might slip again. I looked up and saw the cliff edge; it was so close I could almost touch it. I tried to imagine planting a flag on the top, of people taking my picture to go on the front page of newspapers around the world.

"I'm Amelia Hester McLeod, the great mountaineer!" I yelled.

I grabbed the rail again and pulled myself up the last few steps and over the top of the grassy cliffs. The blizzard had stopped but the sky hung bright and heavy and I could still taste the snow. I lay in the grass shivering, my heart hammering in my chest.

# Chapter 23

I must have fallen asleep because the next sound I heard wasn't the squawk of puffins, or the chirping of fluffy pufflings, or even the roar of the sea. It was the sound of a car — it was Da. He had found me! When the jeep stopped, Da's heavy boots swung out of the car. I wanted to rush over to him and have him wrap his arms tight around me and squeeze me until I felt like I couldn't breathe. But then I saw his face.

It was worse than the face he had when Grandpa first got lost on his way back from the shops. It was worse than the face he had when mean Miss Stokes said I was unteachable. I'd only seen Da with that angry, sad face once before: on the day Mum left.

Da wouldn't talk to me the whole way back. He wouldn't even look at me. When we got home it was even worse. I could see the answer phone blinking: it was filled with messages. Da pressed the button on the voicemail and the messages started to pour out.

"Mr McLeod, this is Miss Rutherford, the head teacher at Bridlebaine Academy. It appears that your daughter Amelia has left the school grounds after an incident with another student. We have sent the pastoral team to look for her, but it's possible she may have taken a ferry back home. Please can you call me at your earliest convenience?"

"Hello, Mr McLeod? This is Miss Archibald, the head of Learning Support. I think we need to have a talk about Amelia's behaviour and progress at Bridlebaine."

"Amelia, are you there? It's Tom. Where are you? Everyone's been out looking for you. Let me know you're OK."

The messages kept coming, but I couldn't listen to any more of them. I just wanted Da to look at me. I needed to explain everything.

"I've been driving all over the island looking for you," Da said. His voice was hoarse like he'd been shouting my name for hours. His eyes were red as if he'd been crying, too. "You know what I thought when I heard you were missing? I thought—" His voice trailed away.

He didn't have to finish. I knew exactly what he'd been thinking. That I'd run off for good just like Mum had.

"It's not all my fault," I started. "I didn't run away from school. It's like I've been trying to tell you, I disappeared!"

But before I could explain any further, Da held up his hand.

"I don't want to hear it, Amelia. I really don't! I stupidly thought that things were getting better. That you were improving at school, making friends. But I was wrong."

I wanted to tell him that I had been trying at school, that I *had* been making friends. It's just that amazing and terrifying things were happening to me too. But I could see Da's eyes glaze over. So I just stared at my shoes and waited for him to get angry. To ground me, or tell me off, or for us to have one of our great house-shaking rows. But Da just rubbed his forehead and covered his eyes.

"You know, for the first time I'm glad your nanna's not around. If she saw this…" Da's voice trailed off again.

But he didn't need to say anything else. I knew

he meant she would be disappointed in me. I had been so bad I had not only disappointed Da, but I had managed to disappoint someone who wasn't even alive any more. I wondered what Mum would think of me.

"Go to bed, Amelia," he said. "I just can't look at you any more."

I slammed the kitchen door behind me, startling Grandpa out his chair. But I didn't care. I thumped my way up the stairs and threw myself into bed. But I wasn't really angry, just sad. I lay in the darkness, unable to sleep. Everything that had happened spun around and around in my head: the fight with Blair, Tom's lies, and the terror of scaling Puffin Cliffs. The scrapes and bruises on my arm still hurt, but not nearly as much as the ache in my chest from Da's words. No matter how hard I tried I couldn't get them to fade away. I cuddled into Pipi's soft white fur and waited for him to come up and check on me. But that night, for the very first time, he didn't.

# Chapter 24

A letter came two days later. It dropped on to the doormat like an unexploded bomb. I looked at the thistle logo and the official-looking type and knew it was from the school. I didn't have to open it to know what it would say. I had stood in the head teacher's chilly office the day before. Miss Rutherford hadn't been nice like the first time we'd met. Instead she had gone on and on about behaviour and expectations. Then she had walked around her desk several times, the bangles on her wrist jangling up and down, before she said it.

*Suspended*.

Da's face had crumpled.

"But I don't want Amelia missing any more school,

I don't want her falling any further behind. I was really hoping that this school would provide her with the support she needed. I know she struggles with her reading and writing but she really is very bright," he said.

"I agree Amelia has a very keen intellect, but there have to be consequences for her actions," Miss Archibald said, wiping her glasses sadly.

I glared at Miss Archibald, trying with all my might to summon a lightning bolt that would set her hair on fire.

"It's no good giving Miss Archibald that look; it's only down to her protests that you haven't been expelled," Miss Rutherford said.

"Amelia Hester McLeod, you will be giving no one dirty looks here. It's you who's at fault," Da said, turning on me.

I folded my arms to show I didn't care, but I couldn't help but wince at him using my full name.

"Did you hear what Miss Rutherford said? You were nearly expelled!"

Miss Rutherford nodded and added, "It's not just the trespassing and fighting we had to take into consideration, which on its own goes against everything that is expected of Bridlebaine Academy's students. It's the very serious matter of Amelia leaving the school grounds unsupervised and without permission." She folded her heavy ringed fingers together and stared up at me from her desk. "Yes, I was all set to make my very first expulsion," Miss Rutherford finished in a very disappointed voice.

"But we decided it would be a shame to lose a pupil like Amelia, who up to this point has shown no bad behaviour," Miss Archibald chimed in.

I folded my arms tighter across my chest. I wasn't going to thank Miss Archibald for saving me, not when it was her fault I was in trouble in the first place.

"What I would like to know is how on earth you managed to get out of the school gates? They're locked in the daytime," Miss Rutherford added.

I held my breath and looked at Miss Archibald, who shifted uncomfortably in her chair. I was certain she had seen me disappear before her glasses were knocked off by the streaming crowd of kids. She opened her mouth to say something but then stopped herself and shook her head.

"Well?" Miss Rutherford clicked her tongue.

I murmured something about climbing the ivy, running along the castle wall and flipping over the top of the gates. All of which would have taken the skill of an Olympic gymnastics champion to pull off. Miss Archibald gave me one of her pointed looks over the top of her glasses. But nobody asked any more questions. It's funny how easily people believe lies over the truth.

My suspension crawled by. Tom rang nearly every day and left long-winded messages about all the devious things Blair was getting up to. But I didn't call him back and when he stopped by, I hid under the kitchen table. He peered through the letterbox and then pushed a card through the door. But I didn't even look at it. I just shoved it under my bed along with the broken compass. I had had enough of the trouble Tom and the disappearing had got me into.

My suspension ended just as the Christmas holidays started but nothing changed. Da remained just as frosty. He didn't even seem that bothered about Christmas. And Christmas had always been Da's favourite time of year. Every year he would dress up like Father Christmas. He'd pull on the old red cap and do his whole "have you been good or bad this year?" routine. And even though I was now too old for it, seeing Da running around in red pyjamas with a pillow up his top always put me in hysterics. But this year Da couldn't even be bothered to wear his Santa cap. Or make mince pies. He didn't even want to help me and Grandpa put up Christmas decorations. Usually there were so many lights strung up that it was likely that our house was visible from space. But this year all we had was a little plastic tree. It was stuck next to the cooker in the kitchen where its fake needles curled up from the heat. I had tried to hang Grandma's special glass baubles on it but they were too heavy and kept falling off. Grandpa had tried to put up some tinsel, but Pipi had eaten half of it. She had gone around burping up glittery bits and whining, so eventually me and Grandpa gave up. No amount of decorations could have made me feel Christmassy anyway. Not with the way Da was acting. He had barely said a word to me since we had come back from the head teacher's meeting. He had spent every moment since then banging doors, and getting up and leaving the room when I came in. I wasn't sure if Da was angry, or disappointed, or if he really just didn't want to be around me any more. It made me feel so confused and I wasn't the only one.

"Are we playing a game?" Grandpa said, after another of our awkward, quiet dinners.

Da didn't roll his eyes with me like usual. Instead he went into the living room and turned the TV up loud. I could hear him flicking through channels. There was the roar of a game-show audience and then the tinkly music of a crime show and then it settled on the sound of David Attenborough's voice narrating a wildlife programme. I wanted to go and curl up on the couch and watch it with him. But I knew I couldn't. Because even though Da was only in the other room, it felt like he was on the other side of the world.

# Chapter 25

When I finally returned to school in January, the days had become shorter. It was dark when I left home and even darker when I came back. The weather had changed too. It hadn't snowed again like the day at Puffin Cliffs. But it stormed constantly. If it wasn't pouring with rain, the wind was whistling down the corridors at school, blowing doors open and thumping against the windows. It was like the outside wanted to get in.

It was a relief to be inside even if it did mean I had to sit through our start of term assembly. I lined up with the rest of my year and we were shepherded to the front of the hall by Mr McNair. As we took our seats I tried to remember how excited I had been the first time I saw the great hall. I had seen the swords mounted above the stage and thought I'd be learning to fence, and looking after eagles and wildcats or learning how to sing and dance whilst someone played the grand piano in a top hat. I mean, I knew that some of that had been a long shot, but I had thought I'd at least make some friends. I looked at Tom. He was drumming his legs against the floor again. I knew having to be quiet and sit still made Tom all twitchy and anxious. But I didn't care any more because as far as I was concerned Tom and me were enemies.

"Welcome back," Miss Rutherford said, taking centre stage. "I hope you have all had a good Christmas holiday."

Mine had been horrible. It had been the worst Christmas since Mum left. Even when Da tried to make an effort, things had gone all wrong. The turkey had been all burnt and the Christmas pudding had gone soggy in the middle. Pipi ended up eating more of it then I did. And even when we gave each other presents it had been a disaster. Grandpa ended up eating all his chocolate liqueurs at once and falling asleep for the rest of the afternoon and all of the evening. The gold necklace Da gave me ended up getting tangled up in my hair and the star pendant got pulled off the chain. But I hadn't cared because I was sure Da was going to love my present. I had made him an amazing model ship, with real rigging and tiny sailor figures. But Da had opened his present the wrong way up and the ship had fallen out of the box. The mast snapped in half and all the little sailors fell off. We had glued the pieces back together, but when it dried it didn't look quite right. It was like me and Da. No matter how I tried to fix things there were all these invisible cracks that couldn't be mended.

"In this new academic term we have many things to look forward to. And looking ahead to the end of the year we have our big summer assembly. A chance to celebrate our accomplishments with teachers and parents. I know many of you like to have the opportunity to take part in this assembly, so teachers from each class and year group will submit a number of names to be drawn at random. So in order to have plenty of time for you to plan your speeches, dances, art exhibits and musical numbers, we will be picking our year group class representatives today," Miss Rutherford said as she clapped her bony hands together to usher forth Mr Todd carrying a box with *Assembly Readers* printed on front of it.

I groaned – there were six year groups and dozens of classes. This was going to take for ever.

"The year seven English Lit class representative will be Chloe Baines," Miss Rutherford read out.

Chloe got up and Blair and the other ponytail gang all whooped. Everyone joined in clapping and Mr Norris, our English teacher, leant over and gave Chloe an excited handshake like she had won the Olympics.

"The year seven art representative will be Ted Smith."

A nervous boy with a very round face got up. I was a little bit surprised it wasn't Tom. But then Tom hadn't always listened to Miss Iris. He had drawn his self-portrait like he was a superhero when we were meant to be drawing a real likeness of ourselves from photos. He'd given himself a mask and everything. Miss Iris hadn't been pleased.

"The year seven representative from Miss Archibald's STAR group will be…" Miss Rutherford continued unfolding the rest of the paper.

I waited for Miss Rutherford to read Ian or Gregory's name out.

"Amelia McLeod."

The whole assembly turned to face me. Everyone knew who I was after Blair's efforts to get the whole school spying on me and Tom.

"Well, get up then," the girl next to me hissed.

I stumbled to my feet. There was a ripple of whispers and then a smattering of polite applause. I sat down again wondering what had just happened. Miss Archibald had told our class we could volunteer and I definitely hadn't put my name in the goldfish bowl. Had she decided to put my name forward anyway? And why would she? She knew I struggled with reading and she knew it was even harder for me when I had to do it in front of people. I suddenly felt very dizzy.

It wasn't long until I found out what had happened. Blair, Chloe and the rest of the ponytail gang were all waiting for me outside the hall. They all looked smug, except Chloe who mouthed "Sorry" at me.

"Congratulations, Amelia. Oh, I hope you didn't mind me putting your name in. I knew you would be too shy to volunteer, so I did it for you," Blair said, giving me a smile that made her look like a satisfied toad.

I tried to walk away. I was determined not to show Blair how upset I was. But she wasn't having any of it.

"Aren't you going to thank me?" she said, putting an arm around my shoulder like we were best mates. "My mum says it's always best to face our fears. And I know what you're afraid of most of all, and that's reading in front of people. You're so terrible at it." Blair smirked.

Blair wasn't wrong. Even after all the terrifying things that had happened with the disappearing, the thought of having to read out in front of people made me feel sick to my stomach.

"I've seen you in class, mouthing all your words, having Miss Archibald help you sound things out. Having to use your special coloured sheets and then still stuttering and spluttering all over the place when you try and read aloud. Just imagine doing that on stage with the whole school laughing at you. Enough to make anyone want to vanish. But especially you, right? Because you're the girl that disappears, aren't you?" Blair said, tightening her arm around me.

"Blair Watson!" I heard Miss Archibald shout from behind us. "What are you and your friends doing?"

Blair turned her grip on my shoulder to a hearty pat.

"I was just congratulating our class reader Miss," Blair said, switching to her sugary sweet little girl voice.

Over the tops of her glasses, Miss Archibald narrowed her eyes.

"Your hair looks nice today. Doesn't it, girls?" Blair said, managing to keep a straight face as she twisted the purple bow at the end of her perfect braid.

The ponytail gang all smirked at Miss Archibald's frizzy bird's nest.

"All right, enough!" Miss Archibald snapped. "Get off to your class before I give you all detention."

Blair walked off with Chloe and the rest of her

cronies. All of them walked perfectly in step, their purple bows bobbing up and down together, before they disappeared around the corner, leaving me and Miss Archibald alone.

"Amelia, did you really put your name up for the assembly? Because it doesn't seem like something you would do. So I was wondering if there was something you wanted to tell me?" Miss Archibald asked.

For just a moment I wanted to tell Miss Archibald everything, but I couldn't. Every time I tried to tell somebody the truth before, everything went wrong. I told all my secrets to Tom and he'd betrayed me. I tried to tell Da the truth and I'd only made him more angry, and I had tried to tell my mum how much I missed her, but ended up driving her away. So I just shook my head.

"Amelia, I know you haven't had the easiest transition into school life. But I wasn't lying when I said I didn't want to lose such a bright intellect from Bridlebaine. So I do hope you feel you can come to me with any problems," Miss Archibald said, putting a hand gently on my shoulder. "No matter how unusual..." she added, giving me the same curious look she had given me back in Miss Rutherford's office.

I stared at my feet. I felt that if I looked up at her I would burst into a million tears.

"All right, Amelia. I won't keep you," Miss Archibald sighed.

I just managed to make it to the girls' loos before I was flooded by a tsunami of tears.

"Amelia," I heard Tom's voice as the bathroom door flew open.

"Go away!" I yelled, slamming the toilet door and locking it.

"What happened in assembly, why did your name get picked out to read?" Tom asked, trying to peep at me from under the door.

"It's none of your business, not after what you did!"

"I know what I did was awful. I should have told the truth. I should have stuck up for you," Tom said. "But I got scared. I was terrified my parents would ground me again. But worse: I got scared my gran would sell the ponies just like she said she would. I love those ponies, Amelia – I didn't know what else to do."

I sniffed.

"I shouldn't have done it. But I've got something to make it up to you."

I wondered if Tom had kept his promise, if he had used his sleuthing skills to find where my mum was living now. So when Tom slid the book of myths from Mr Sinclair's shop under the toilet door, my heart sank.

"I've been helping Mr Sinclair all Christmas. He made me do the most awful stuff, like set mouse traps and clean spiderwebs off the high shelves and alphabetize all the romance books. But just after Christmas we started reordering the books in the secret bit behind the red curtain and I was able to smuggle the myth book out. So now we can give back your wish and transfer your scary powers back to the Serpent's Tooth Rock and save the island!" Tom finished breathlessly.

But I didn't care about giving back my powers and saving the island. Because Da had been wrong, I wasn't a proper islander, I didn't belong on a cold dark island where I was the stupid kid with no friends. I was Amelia Hester McLeod, named after two great pioneering explorers. And I belonged with my mum, fighting crocodiles down the Amazon, or riding camels through the desert, or even dodging polar bears in the arctic.

I slid the book back under the toilet door. Because Blair was right: I was the girl who disappeared and it was time I started acting like it.

# Chapter 26

That night I felt the tingling in my hand grow stronger. It was like I had summoned my powers back. All I needed to do was figure out how to get them to make me disappear again and I was sure that they would fulfil my wish: I would get to be with Mum. I couldn't sleep thinking about it, so I pulled out the blue exercise book from my bag.

I turned to a fresh page and wrote:

Dear Mum,

Here are all the things we are going to do when we live together.

- Go camping out in Africa like Mary Henrietta Kingsley. (This time I promise not to be scared of snakes.)
- Sail around the world in a real ship hopping from island to island and finding all kinds of treasure like the pirate Anne Bonny.
- Conquer Mount Everest against all the odds, just like Junko Tabei.
- Fly across the world like Amelia Earhart.
- Travel across the desert by Arab stallion like Lady Hester Stanhope.

The rest of the week of school crawled by. Tom kept trying to find ways to talk to me and Blair continued to stalk me in the hallways. But Da was starting to make a bit more effort. He even made me frittata for dinner again. But my mind was made up. When the weekend came, I was going to disappear again, and this time off this island for good.

But by Saturday Grandpa was having another of his funny mornings. He'd been in the living room, sitting in the big old-fashioned green armchair and repeating,

"Oh dear, oh dear."

I suspected he was thinking about more unlikely ways he could pop his clogs. But when I asked him what the matter was, he muttered, "Things need to be put right, if only I could remember how they did it last time."

I had no idea who "they" were, so I made us both a cup of tea and fetched him Da's not-so-secret stash of ginger biscuits from under the sink.

"It's a horrible thing, getting old, Amelia. I hardly think it's worth the bother any more," Grandpa said.

"Grandpa, I know you're going to live to a hundred so you can get your letter from the queen," I said, passing Grandpa his mug of tea.

"You're very special, Amelia, you know that?" Grandpa said, as he brushed my knotty hair out of my eyes.

I frowned and stared down at the toe sticking out from the hole in my sock. I didn't think I was particularly special. I wasn't good at school or popular and seemed to do nothing but disappoint Da.

"Your grandma would be so proud of you," Grandpa added.

A wave of sadness crashed over me. I held the biscuit I'd dunked in my tea a moment too long, and it fell apart into the mug.

"How about you and me play a game of chess then?" Grandpa asked, wiggling in the armchair so he could pull his trousers up over his belly, before he got up, went over to the desk and pulled out the chess set he'd made me for my ninth birthday.

Grandpa's brilliant at making things but he's never been any good at playing chess, even before he got so forgetful. He calls the knight the horsey and both of us would abandon the rules halfway through. We'd just end up throwing the pieces at each other whilst yelling "bombs away". It's much more fun than normal chess. But even so, I couldn't stay. I felt the tingling in my hand calling me. I kissed him on top of his bald head and made for the stairs. If I went to live with Mum, Da would have more time to look after Grandpa, I thought. But it didn't untie the knot in my stomach.

I could hear Da rattling around upstairs. If I stayed in my room there was every possibility he would pop in to check I was doing my homework. I couldn't risk him seeing me in the middle of my great disappearing act. So I tiptoed out into the corridor that led to the attic room. I stepped carefully on to the attic stairs, testing each one to find the non-squeaky bit, so as not to alert Da. But it was no good. No matter how careful I was, the stairs still creaked with every painfully slow footstep.

Squeak…

Squeak…

Squeak!

When I was halfway up, I heard the sound of Da's bedroom door flying open. I froze and my heart started to thump heavily. Then I heard it close, so I darted up the few remaining steps and turned the handle into the attic room.

The attic room was just as Mum left it. There was a large wooden bed still made up with the fresh sheets, a wardrobe filled with a few of her shirts and dresses and an old Japanese tea chest filled with her books: lots of biographies of terribly important people, travel books and romance books with embarrassing titles. Under the beams at the end of the room was a big round window that looked out to the sea. When I was little Mum and I had watched for Da's boat out of the window… It was a beautiful room. But me and Da never used it for anything, because every corner of it still felt so full of Mum. It was surely the perfect place to try and summon the disappearing to take me to her.

I squeezed my hand, closed my eyes and whispered: "I want to disappear…"

I heard a rustle and the door creaked open. My heart jumped. But it was just Pipi. She had followed me up, her tail between her legs. Whatever I was doing, she was already sure she didn't like it.

"I want to disappear," I said again, closing my eyes. I waited for the room to flicker and for the sound of the pop in my ear, but all I could hear was the roar of the wind outside.

"I want to disappear," I said again, stretching my arms out as if I was about to take flight.

But still nothing happened. Pipi looked up at me with her head half cocked.

*Woof!* she barked.

Even she thought I looked stupid.

I sat down on the end of my bed trying to figure out what I was doing wrong. I had only been able to deliberately make the disappearing work twice. Once in the bookshop and once when Miss Archibald and Tom were chasing after me at school. And even back then I hadn't known how I was doing it, it just sort of happened. Maybe if I looked at all the things I had found it would help me? Over Christmas I had moved them up to the attic. I felt like they belonged in Mum's room with all the things she had left behind in her old tea trunk. One by one I pulled them out:

- The binoculars I found on Sometimes Island
- The fossil that Da donated to the "Wonders of the Island" school display case
- The pirate flag I found in *The Bonny*
- The piece of sea-worn glass that I found in Puffin Cave

Finally, I pulled out Mum's compass. The cracked glass glinted and the broken needle wouldn't move from pointing south. But it didn't matter, because Mum's initials were still untouched on the back of the gold case. I ran my finger over them and remembered how I had made myself disappear at school. I hadn't just wished to disappear; I'd been thinking about Mum first.

"Take me to Mum," I whispered and my hand grew hotter and the needle on the compass started to spin.

"It's working!" I gasped.

There was a rumble of thunder. The sky turned white with lightning and then everything fell into darkness. I thought of my broken promise to Tom and the inky dark stormy drawings in the pages of the book. But I couldn't stop now.

"Take me to Mum," I said again and the needle flew faster.

Pipi growled deep in her throat. But I wouldn't stop, I couldn't.

"Take me to Mum!" I roared.

The room flickered, Pipi howled, and then everything went wrong.

# Chapter 27

A lot of things happened next. Firstly, there was an almighty crack of thunder that rocked the whole house. Secondly, Pipi bit me. Not just a nip, or a nibble but a proper sinking of her teeth into my ankle.

"Ow!" I yelled over the roll of thunder.

But Pipi wouldn't let go. She was trying to stop me disappearing by any means possible. I tried to pull her off. But it was too late, my foot disappeared. And then my leg and my torso and then my ears popped. And I was gone.

When my eyes snapped open, I was lying face down on attic floorboards. I groaned. I hadn't gone anywhere. Pipi had interrupted the magic and caused the disappearing to halt.

"You're a bad dog, a very bad dog," I told her, while turning over and rubbing my sore ankle.

But as I sat up I could see everything was different. I was definitely in an attic, but it wasn't my attic. My heart leaped with excitement. Maybe this was the attic of the place where Mum lived; maybe the magic had finally brought me to her.

"Mum!" I called out wildly.

But nobody answered and as I looked around this seemed less and less like a place my Mum might live. All around me were piles and piles of old newspapers, cracked mirrors, bits of what looked like old bicycle parts, and old furniture. And the walls were covered in frames filled with butterflies and insects and creepy crawlies. I sat up shakily and knocked over a dusty lamp.

"Did you hear something?" a voice from downstairs called.

"Probably owls again trying to make a nest in all that junk you keep up there," another voice replied.

I knew those voices! I shuddered, because of all the places to disappear to, this was the very worst! I was in Hettie and Penny's attic.

I grabbed for my compass but it wasn't in my hand, or my pocket. I must have dropped it. I searched around the floor and then I heard a growl. Pipi had it in her mouth, hanging from the tattered ribbon.

"Pipi, give it back. We have to get out of here," I said, reaching out for it.

Pipi barked and shot across the room, knocking into furniture and boxes, and with a great thud she toppled over the dressmaker's dummy. A huge cloud of dust flew up around us.

"What on earth is going on up there?" Hettie cried.

I threw myself across the room and grabbed Pipi just as I heard the creak on the staircase. With a startled yap, Pipi dropped the compass. It skidded across the floor. The footsteps got louder. There was no time to grab the compass but I couldn't leave without it. I was going to have to hide. I looked around desperately: behind me there was an old wardrobe. I managed to pull the door closed behind us just as Hettie and Penny burst in. I put a hand over Pipi's muzzle but she managed to squeak out a whimper.

"Do you think we have mice up here?" Penny asked.

"I wouldn't be surprised if we had all sorts of creatures living up here. I mean, look at this mess! Didn't you tell me you had organized this? I mean, what do we need this for?" Hettie said, picking up a hedgehog-shaped boot scraper. "And what are we keeping that old wardrobe for? Between us we don't have enough clothes to fill the one downstairs."

I held my breath. Through the crack in the door I could see Hettie's slippered feet getting closer and closer. The floorboards squeaked and with every footstep the cupboard door creaked open just a little more. I was going to be discovered and there was no way I could explain how I had found myself in Hettie and Penny's attic.

I could see the compass glinting by the old mannequin. But I couldn't get to it, not without being seen. I squeezed my eyes shut and tried to think up a super-amazing escape plan. Mum would tell me that all great explorers had to make full use of their surroundings to survive. Just like Ada Blackjack who had lived for two years as a castaway on an uninhabited frozen island. She had survived by catching small animals and using their fur to keep her warm. But I was in a closet. All I had was some holey dresses and a dusty old fur coat. But thinking about Ada Blackjack had given me an idea. I pulled the fur coat down from the hanger as quietly as I could and wrapped myself and Pipi in it. If this was going to work, I thought, I would have to take Mr Todd our drama teacher's advice. I would have to commit to the part.

As soon as I saw Hettie and Penny's feet at the door I leaped out of the closet, howling. Pipi joined in, growling in the back of her throat. Between the two of us we sounded like a hideous bear/dog monster.

Penny screamed and Hettie fell over.

"Raaaarrr!" I cried, getting carried away, before grabbing the compass and running for the door.

With the coat over my head I couldn't see where I was going. I tumbled down the stairs, crashed through a door and lay panting on the floor. Pipi wriggled out of the coat. But the buttons had got all tangled up in my hair. I tore at it, spinning around and knocking into things. I heard a loud crash and then the thump of something heavy falling over. And then with a yank the coat was finally pulled from my head.

Hettie and Penny loomed over me. I expected them to be surprised or even angry. But Penny just sighed and, even more surprisingly, Hettie smiled.

"I was wondering when you were going to show up," she said.

# chapter 28

"We have a lot to talk about and not very much time to do it," Hettie said as she picked up the lamp and chair I had knocked over and put them back in place.

I looked around. Even in the dim light I could see that Hettie and Penny's house was completely different to how I had imagined it. Under the fur coat, I was sure I had been running through a house of horrors, of stuffed animals and portraits of stern old relatives. But it wasn't like that at all. It was filled with bright paintings, mismatched home-made cushions and cosy-looking armchairs. Even so, I didn't want to be sitting in Hettie and Penny's living room. I didn't want to be having another scary confusing chat with them, and I definitely didn't want to be drinking the strange green tea that Hettie had given me. But Pipi was curled up happily on Penny's lap, and even though she had been a very bad dog, I couldn't go home without her.

"That wish you made, Amelia – it puts us all in danger," Hettie said.

I opened my mouth to protest again about not making a wish. But Hettie raised her hand.

"I may be old, but I'm no fool. I know it was your birthday before the rock disappeared. I know you and that new boy have been running around trying to steal the book of island myths. And I know you couldn't get up into my attic without some sort of strange magic."

"How do you know all this?" I said.

Hettie looked at me; her strange yellow eyes glinted in the dark.

"You don't think you're the only one to have made a wish that came true, do you?" she said.

Suddenly everything made sense. Hettie and Penny's visits. The warnings. Knowing exactly which book me and Tom had taken. I had a million questions I wanted to ask. But one was more important than all the others.

"What did you wish for?" I whispered.

Hettie sighed.

"On my eleventh birthday, Amelia, I wished to be popular. I'd had enough of feeling different. Of always being teased and finding myself left out. Instead I wanted lots of friends, to be invited to all the parties and to never have to sit on my own. I wanted to belong."

My eyes met her odd-coloured ones. I couldn't imagine Hettie wanting to fit in. But then again, I couldn't imagine Hettie as an eleven-year-old girl either.

"Did it work?" I asked.

"Oh, at first nothing happened. Just like you, I thought that making a wish and touching the rock was just a silly island tradition. But then small things began to happen."

"Like what?" I asked.

"Things like my hair didn't do the curly sticking-up thing at the back," Hettie said pointing to her messy bun. "And then my spots disappeared, and the crook in my nose seemed to flatten out."

"And your eyes, don't forget your eyes," Penny said.

"My eyes. They didn't stand out any more. They weren't this strange yellow colour; they turned a hazel brown," Hettie said. "And the more I seemed to change, the more all the boys started to notice me and the girls wanted to be friends with me."

I tried to picture Hettie young and beautiful and without her strange yellow witch eyes. I wondered if I would have wanted to be friends with her too.

"She got invited to the top table in lunch. Where all the popular girls sat," Penny added.

I thought of the lunch table where Blair and her friends held court. It was huge. They even had extra chairs for their bags. But no one dared try to sit there unless they were invited by Blair.

"And then other things began to happen too. I won the sports day cup. I'd never run a race before, but my legs just seemed to fly around the track. And I found myself auditioning for the school play and being given the lead role – I would never have stood up on stage before in front of hundreds of people, *never*.

"But being one of the popular crowd actually turned out to be really lonely. There were all these new rules I had to follow to fit in: I couldn't let my mum walk me to school and I couldn't work in my grandma's knitting shop at the weekend."

"And she couldn't keep company with me any more," Penny said.

I couldn't imagine Hettie without Penny. It seemed totally mad that there had ever been a time when they hadn't been together.

"And the more popular I became, the worse the

weather grew," Hettie carried on. "And just before the school play, a terrible storm hit."

"The storm that everyone still remembers, even your grandpa. It was the one that ripped the roof from the church and nearly destroyed every house on this island," Penny added.

"If it wasn't for Penny helping me take back my wish there wouldn't be any island left," Hettie said. "She came across the old book of myths in Sinclair's and together we commandeered a boat to sail out to where the rock was submerged and summon it back."

"But what about having the lead role in the play and being popular? Weren't you worried that all of that would be taken away from you?" I asked in a small voice, thinking how hard I had tried to fit in. How much I had wanted to make friends and do well in school so Da could have been proud of me. And how it had all gone horribly wrong.

Hettie shook her head.

"I realized being popular wasn't nearly as important as all the things I already had. And it definitely wasn't worth losing them over," she said, taking Penny's hand.

"That's the funny thing about wishes, Amelia: we make them because we think we want them, but it rarely works out that simply," Penny added.

"So let us help you put a stop to this," Hettie said,

"before you find yourself in a situation that will make you unhappy for ever."

"No!" I said, shoving the table back, grabbing hold of Pipi and running from the cottage.

Because Penny was wrong. Maybe Hettie's wish hadn't been what she truly wanted, but mine was. My wish was going to take me to Mum, to where I really belonged. I wasn't ready to give that up. Not when it felt so close to coming true.

# Chapter 29

That night I fell into bed. I was too tired to disappear again. That, and I couldn't get Hettie and Penny's story out of my head. I listened to the house creak and groan in the wind and slipped Mum's compass under my pillow. Pipi growled when she saw it. But it wasn't the fierce growl I had heard up in the attic; it was her normal doggy growl, the one she used when she was scared by strangers or the vacuum cleaner. My ankle was still sore from where she had bitten it. Pipi whined and licked my hand when she saw me rub it in bed. I knew she was trying to apologize. I wasn't cross any more: I understood that she didn't want me to face danger like I had on Sometimes Island. I wished I could explain why I was doing it.

But even though Pipi could tell I was upset faster than any human, she couldn't understand this.

"You're a good dog really," I said, stroking her velvety ears.

With the house quiet and Pipi snoring beside me, I almost wished I could forget about the wish, the storm and Hettie's story. That I could just go back to being boring Amelia, the weird home-schooled girl who never had adventures. But I couldn't. Hettie was right, I had a choice to make and I needed to make it soon.

On Monday morning, Pipi wouldn't let me out of her sight. She pulled at my school trousers and I had to wrestle her for my tie. It was only at breakfast that she calmed down and went to sleep in her basket. But that was only because she peed in my school shoes.

"That won't stop me leaving," I told her as I pulled on the new pair of yellow wellies Da had bought me. I shrugged on my yellow mac, opened the door and gasped.

The snow had all come down in one heavy sheet: everything was white. The ground was white, the sky was white, even the sea seemed to have changed colour. The snow lay so thick that I could hear the rooftops groaning with the weight of it. I'd never seen the island look so still. Pipi put one paw into the snow, barked and bolted back inside the house.

It took me ages to get to the harbour. The snow sunk over the top of my yellow wellies as I slowly struggled through it. I could see a couple of kids tobogganing down in a sled. One girl was even wearing snowshoes. Everyone else had arrived in their parents' trucks and jeeps. But no one was getting on the ferry. The captain was yelling something from the deck but I couldn't hear because the church bell wouldn't stop ringing.

"What's going on?" I asked the group of girls in front.

Blair's awful friends turned around, their faces white moons under their matching woolly bobble hats. But this time no one made fun of me or told me off for being stupid. Even Blair was too busy trying to listen to what the ferry captain was trying to say.

"Storm warning," Chloe whispered.

I tried not to think about the inky illustration of the storm from the book of myths. Especially not of the picture of the island sinking into the sea.

"No ferry today. The school is closed," the captain managed to finally shout over the bells.

But nobody clapped or high-fived each other; no one seemed even a bit excited. Not when all the adults looked so frightened. Tom was staring out to sea watching the dark waves crash against the harbour.

229

I knew he was thinking of the page from the book where the sea had swallowed up the island. I thought about Hettie and Penny's story and looked up at the church with no roof. But I could feel Mum's compass in my pocket. I gripped it tighter and felt the warmth grow in my hand. Just one more time couldn't hurt, could it? I could come back. I could return the powers to the rock and fix everything after I found Mum.

I closed my eyes and muttered into the roar of the waves and the ringing of the bells:

"Take me to Mum…"

# Chapter 30

Before I even opened my eyes I knew I was in trouble. I could hear the roar of waves and the sound of the bell ringing louder than ever. But it wasn't the sound of the church bells. It was the tinkle of Da's lucky ship bell. I blinked. I was on the deck of Da's boat, and in the wind and waves it was trying to pull free of its moorings.

I struggled up just as a huge wave buffeted the side and poured over the deck. I gripped the side and stared out into the harbour. A dozen other boats had drifted out on to the sea. A couple had huge gashes ripped across their bows. One made a horrible gurgling noise as it began to sink. I leaned over the other side; Da's boat hadn't drifted too far yet. I could still reach the ladder back on to the dock; I could still make it back to shore. Back to safety. But why had the magic made me disappear and brought me here? This wasn't where Mum was, and the disappointment crashed into me like one of the high waves.

I felt the boat rock again and the rope shuddered. I screwed my eyes closed and thought of Laura Dekker from New Zealand, the young girl who set off alone to sail around the world. At thirteen she made her plans to leave, throwing her school books over the side of her yacht and writing a farewell note to her father. But she had been stopped by the police so it wouldn't be until she was fourteen that she finally managed to set sail. And then nothing prevented her from making her trip around the world. Not bad weather or even the threat of pirates on the open sea. I knew there was no way she would have abandoned her mission. She had travelled the world in 518 days. I just had to survive long enough to find one last clue.

I pulled myself up just as another huge wave crashed over the boat. The boat bucked up into the air, lobster pots flew across the deck. But this time I didn't stop. I didn't even look back. I tugged myself forward and up into the cabin and steadied myself on the wheel. And that's when I saw it: Da's red lockbox, where he kept his money, maps and a great big pocket knife. Da always kept it locked for safety, but this time the key was swinging from the lock, like it was waiting for me to turn it. I reached out with trembling hands. Whatever was inside this box was important. I could feel it. I turned the key.

Click.

The box sprang open and inside I saw a letter addressed to me. What was Da doing with a letter for me? Was it one from the school? I pulled it out and stared at it. My name was written in swoopy, scratchy handwriting. There was only one person who wrote like that: Mum. The boat rocked again and the mooring rope groaned. But it didn't matter. I couldn't wait a moment longer. I ripped the letter open.

Dear Amelia,

I'm hoping this reaches you for your birthday. The lady in the post office said putting extra stamps on it wouldn't make it get there any faster. But I've stuck a few more on, just in case.

I know your eleventh birthday is an important one. Your da is probably going to take you out to Serpent's Tooth Rock to make a wish. I wish I could be there to watch you become a proper islander, but I know I've made a mess of things.

Da told me how upset you got after I tried to call you last time. How you ran away so you didn't have to speak to me.

I hate thinking that I could upset you so much. Especially when I've thrown both you and your father's lives upside down. I wanted to call so many times but I didn't know what to say to make things better. So I thought that for a little while both of you would be better off without me. But I haven't stopped missing you, and I know that I need to explain everything properly. So I thought writing might be better. I know you're not fond of words but sometimes it's easier to write down the things we're not brave enough to say in person.

I know as you're reading this you're probably wondering why I left. That's maybe the hardest thing to explain. I grew up travelling, Amelia. My family were always moving from place to place for my dad's work. And when I grew up I could never settle in one place for long. So whenever I got tired of being in one place, I got up and went on an adventure. Then one day I came to Dark Muir and met your da, and something unexpected and wonderful happened: you. So I moved to this tiny island I had only just heard of, married your da and packed my travelling things away. But life on the island is hard, and after a while I got sad. I missed my family and I hated living so far away from everything. And the more time I lived on the island the sadder I got, and the more me and your da fought. I'm sure you remember the fighting, and for that I'm truly sorry. I kept wanting us to move but this was your da's home and yours too. And when your grandpa came to live with us, I knew we could never leave. So I took another job away from the island. I wanted you to know that when I left I didn't know it would be for good. If I had I would have done everything differently. I thought taking a job away would make things better. That it would give me and your da some time and space to think. But the longer I was away the more I realized how unhappy I had become living on Dark Muir. And then I met Bob while I was filming a documentary in Australia and we fell in love. This year we moved into a flat in Edinburgh. We're both very happy. But that doesn't mean I've stopped loving you, Amelia. Nothing could ever do that.

I know this is a lot to take in, which is why I understand it might take you a while to want to talk to me again. And that's OK, because I will be waiting: I will wait for as long as you need me to.

All my love,

Mum

PS. I hope very much that you like the compass I sent. It was your grandma's and then mine and now on your eleventh birthday, it's yours. I hope it always helps you find your way home.

It was only a short letter but I took a long, long time to read it. I wanted to understand every word. Because surely there had to be a mistake! All this time I had thought that Mum couldn't get in contact because she was on the other side of the world. That she was paragliding in the Andes, or lost in the jungles of Peru searching for Incan treasure, or saving penguins in the Antarctic. But she was just in Edinburgh. So close that I could almost swim to it.

My hand grew hot and I felt Mum's compass shaking in my pocket. I pulled it out. The needle was spinning. With every turn it spun, faster and faster, and my whole body started to tingle. I could feel the disappearing ready at my fingertips more powerful than ever. I knew that this had been the last thing I needed to find. The last place the rock had needed me to go, that now it was ready to fulfil my wish.

But the letter had changed everything.

## Chapter 31

My head was filled with questions. Questions I realized I'd always had but had just forced into the box in my head so I didn't have to think about them. Questions like:

- What had stopped Mum coming back?
- Why had she waited so long to write?
- Why hadn't she taken me with her?

I could feel the power buzzing through me. I was about to get my wish. I should have been thrilled. But my world felt like it had been turned upside down. And the question that burned the most brightly wasn't about Mum, it was about Da:

• Why had he kept the letter from me?

I needed to find out.

I could barely make my way back home from the harbour. Everything looked new and strange in the snow. I could just make out the light from the windows in my house. It took all my strength to make it up through the hill; the wind battered against me and every footstep made me sink deeper and deeper into the snow. But I could see the light from our kitchen window get brighter and brighter. Finally I burst through the door in a hail of snow and ice.

"Amelia," Da said, wrapping his arms around me. "I've been so worried."

Even though it was the first hug I'd had in a long while, I pushed him away. Da dropped his arms, looking hurt.

"I heard school's been cancelled, I was about to go looking for you," he said as the wind outside stormed around our house and made it shake.

Hail clattered against the window, the old oak tree outside creaked and moaned and a deep roll of thunder rippled across the island. But the storm wasn't just outside any more; it was in me.

"Why would you care? You don't even want me around!" I shouted.

The lights went out; a bolt of lightning flashed past the window, illuminating Da's shocked face.

"Amelia, that's not true," he said.

"You're a liar!" I yelled as I pulled the envelope from my pocket and slammed it on to the kitchen table.

The lights came back on and for a moment the house filled with the most deafening silence.

"How did you get that?" Da said.

I shook my head. I wasn't the one who needed to answer any questions. Da sighed and sat down heavily.

"This is not how I wanted this to happen. I wanted to give this to you when you were ready."

"When would that be?" I said, thinking of the months it had sat in the boat lockbox.

"I wanted to give it to you when I gave you the compass, I really did. But I know how much you miss your mum on your birthday and I was scared that if you read the letter you would get upset and…" Da stopped.

But I knew what he was thinking about. I remembered how last time Mum had tried to talk to me on my birthday I had run away. How Da had really thought I was lost and cried when he'd found me. How closely he'd watch me when the phone rang from then on. And how he'd made such a big effort on my last birthday so I wouldn't feel sad. But that didn't stop the horrible stormy feeling in the pit of my stomach.

"You could have given it to me after my birthday," I told him fiercely.

"I was going to when everything settled down at school. But you had such a tricky start and then there was the suspension and I didn't want to make everything worse..." Da trailed off. "I thought I was protecting you."

"But you weren't," I replied, thinking of all the times I missed Mum. All the times I had to invent where she was just so I could make myself feel better by imagining what she was doing at that moment.

"I wanted this to be the year we got on our feet. I thought you becoming an islander and starting school would be our big chance to start over. I didn't want anything to ruin that. But the more the year went on, the more I realized I'd got everything wrong," Da finished and I could see his face break into a million pieces.

But I couldn't look at Da any more. I stormed upstairs.

I could feel the rock's magic buzzing through me. It wanted to take me to Mum and Mum wanted to see me. Didn't she? That's why she had written. She hadn't forgotten about me. She had just been waiting for my letter in reply. But this was going to be even better. I was going to turn up and surprise her. She would be so pleased to see me, wouldn't she? I tried not to think of the months that had gone by without her calling. Or the flat in Edinburgh. Or the man named Bob. I tried not to think about what Da had said. Instead, I packed my backpack full of the things I thought I would need.

- *The Little Book of Lady Adventurers*
- The compass
- Miss Archibald's blue journal book
- And the pair of dinosaur pyjamas I'd managed to secretly wash after my adventure in the bog.

I looked around the room one final time. It made my heart ache to think of leaving, but I couldn't have second thoughts. I closed my eyes and squeezed the compass. I was going to disappear; I was going to have my wish come true. All I had to do was say the words.

"Amelia!" I heard Da cry out.

But I didn't want to hear any more of what he had to say. I'd made up my mind: there was nothing he could do to stop me leaving. But then the door shuddered open and Da stood, ashen-faced.

"Your grandpa's disappeared," he said.

# Chapter 32

I helped Da search the whole house again. But Grandpa wasn't in bed, or sitting in his armchair listening to stories on the radio, and where his boots should have been there was just an empty space.

"He kept muttering something about putting it right. About stopping the storm. But I wasn't really listening," Da said, his head in his hands.

I couldn't stop thinking about Grandpa's "fabulous ways to pop your clogs" list. How nearly everything he said might come true if he was out in this storm. He could be hit by lightning, or drown in a bog, or be killed by an avalanche. And all of it, *all of it,* would be my fault. I had been so wrapped up in making my wish come true that I hadn't thought how it might hurt Da and Grandpa.

"I'm going to go out and find him," Da said, going out into the hall to get his coat and boots.

But I knew the snow was too deep and the blizzard was too fierce to find anyone. There was only one thing that could save Grandpa and that was to use my powers.

If the magic had grown so powerful it was ready to take me to Mum, maybe I could use it just this once to take me somewhere else. I tucked the compass back into my pocket.

"Take me to Grandpa," I whispered, but nothing happened.

I closed my eyes and tried to picture Grandpa's face. His shimmery grey-green eyes, the same as mine and Da's. The way they crinkled up when he laughed and how he cried at silly romantic movies when he thought no one was watching. I felt the familiar tingle in my hand.

"Take me to Grandpa," I said again.

And this time I thought of Grandpa teaching me how to tie my shoelaces, and us getting into fights while playing chess and all the Sunday afternoons we had spent listening to murder mysteries on the radio.

My hand grew hot.

"It's working," I yelled and Pipi howled. "OK, you can come with me, just no biting," I said, scooping her up and putting her into my backpack. She yapped happily. I pulled the strap of my backpack tight as the room started to shimmer.

"Amelia, what are you…" Da said, appearing in the doorway with his coat half-on. I tried to turn around but I couldn't, because my feet had already disappeared. Da's jaw fell open, his face filled with shock.

"Amelia!" he shouted, and I could hear the fear in his voice.

Suddenly I realized I was terrified too, because I was about to head out into a storm with nothing but a broken compass and a dog who was scared of snow. But I couldn't stop what was happening. The magic had grown stronger and it was working faster than ever before. The sound of the ocean roared in my ears as the room flickered away.

"Da," I called back, but my voice sounded so tiny and far away.

Just as the room finally faded away, I felt Da reach out and grab me.

"Don't let go," I squeaked.

"Never," Da replied, hugging me tight, before we both disappeared.

# Chapter 33

"Amelia," I heard someone shout, but the sound of thunder was so loud that my head hurt. Then I felt someone shaking me.

"Amelia," the voice called again.

Then everything that had happened – the storm, Grandpa going missing and the disappearing – all suddenly came flooding back.

"Grandpa," I cried out.

But when I opened my eyes, I saw it wasn't Grandpa who was holding me. It was Da; his eyes were filled with concern and he was trying to say something. I could see his lips moving, but I couldn't hear anything. It was like a bomb had gone off and I was now completely deaf. Then a bolt of lightning hit the ground and everything came roaring back.

"Amelia, we have to get out of this storm," Da yelled and he pulled me to my flickering feet.

I stood shakily and looked around. We were at Sometimes Island: Grandpa's favourite spot and the place I had disappeared to that very first time. But it didn't look anything like how it had the time me and Pipi appeared here in the middle of the night. The cliffs had fallen away, there were uprooted trees everywhere and the rest were being pulled in all directions by the howling wind. The sky crackled, flashed white, and fell into darkness again. I looked around. Grandpa was meant to be here. I was meant to have brought us right to him. Had I made a mistake? Had the disappearing not worked properly this time? Everything felt wrong.

"We have to find Grandpa!" I yelled back and I could hear Pipi barking madly in my backpack.

But Da wouldn't let go. He held my arm tight, and pulled me over to the trees. I remembered the night that me and Pipi had been stranded on the island, how we had heard something chasing us. But the only thing we were being chased by this time was the storm, which roared overhead. The rain lashed my face; the wind pulled me off my feet. I didn't know where we were running to and every part of my body just wanted to stop.

"We have to get to higher ground," Da yelled. "The island's sinking."

I could see darkness rising around us. It was the sea and it was coming in fast.

"You don't understand. I brought us to where Grandpa wandered off to. He's still out here. We have to find him!" I yelled.

Da took me by my shoulders. "Are you absolutely sure?" he asked.

I nodded.

"Stay here. I'll go and look for him."

I shook my head. I didn't want Da to go.

"I won't be long."

I thought of how Mum had said the same thing before she left.

"I don't want you to leave and never come back," I cried.

"Oh, Amelia," Da said, and as he pulled me closer I breathed in the smell of his musty old jacket. "I'm never going to leave you."

I hugged Da back. I'd forgotten how much I missed him. How much I missed his bear hugs and his checking in on me at night. How much I missed his smiley-face breakfast and Da surprise suppers. How could I have ever thought about leaving? I squeezed him harder as the sky crackled with lightning. Then I pulled away.

"I think I know where Grandpa might be," I said.

"Let's go," Da said, slipping his hand into mine.

We raced through the trees over the slippery rocks and up the cliff. All the while I could hear the thunder of the waves breaking around us. We didn't have long. My heart thumped. But through the trees I could see it: the stone circle, glowing with the same strange lights I had heard about on the night the Serpent's Tooth Rock disappeared. There in the middle was Grandpa. But he wasn't moving.

"Grandpa!" I shouted and Pipi leaped from my backpack and we all ran over to him. Pipi licked his face and Grandpa's eyes flickered but didn't open.

"Grandpa, wake up," I whispered, holding his hand as Da wrapped his jacket around his shoulders and Pipi nestled her head under his chin.

If I'd just listened to Tom about returning the powers to the rock, then maybe I could have stopped all of this happening. Because now I had put me and Da in danger and I was going to lose Grandpa and it was all my fault. The storm roared around us. All the birds flew up from the trees, their screeching filling the sky.

I closed my eyes. I just wanted to undo my wish. I wanted everything to go back to the way it was. I reached out and touched the stones. They were hot. Just like Serpent's Tooth Rock had been.

"I promise if Grandpa's OK, I'll make everything right. I'll find a way to take back the wish," I muttered.

The green glow grew brighter around us.

Grandpa's eyes flickered open.

"Did it work?" he asked blearily.

"You stupid old man. What are you doing out here?" Da yelled.

I grabbed Grandpa and Da and pulled them in for a hug. I couldn't stop crying. But I could hear the waves now, louder than ever as they crashed against the cliffs. The island was being swallowed up.

"I'm sorry, this is my all my fault – it's the wish I made that's causing the storm," I said.

"What did you wish for?" Grandpa asked.

"To be with Mum. I just missed her so much and then everything bad happened at school and Da stopped talking to me. I thought I'd messed everything up, that I'd disappointed you so much you'd stopped caring about me. So I'd be better off with Mum."

"Oh, Amelia, I've been so stupid," Da said, shaking his head. "I should have given you the letter. I should have tried harder to let your mum be part of your life. And I should have listened to you when you tried to tell me about what was happening. But if there's one thing you never have to worry about, it's me caring about you. I know I'm not always good at showing it, but I love you, Amelia. I love you when you're funny and silly and I love you when you're filthy and bad-tempered and misbehaving and awful. I love you no matter what."

I had thought Mum was on the other side of the world and Da didn't love me any more. But I finally realized that I'd understood everything backwards.

I pulled out Mum's compass from my pocket. It was still spinning and spinning, wanting to fulfil the wish. But Mum had given me the compass so I could always find home. And home wasn't with her. It was with Da and Grandpa and Pipi, on the house on the hill under the North Star.

I slipped the compass back into my pocket. But this time I didn't need to close my eyes to think of home, because my heart was filled with it. I could see our living room with Grandpa's chess set next to his big comfy armchair and our worn-out leather couch. And I could picture the kitchen filled up with the smells of Da's mighty dinners. And then I saw my bedroom covered in the millions of plastic glow-in-the-dark stars, that me and Da had hung together.

"Ready?" I asked, scooping Pipi back into my bag.

"Ready for what?" Da asked.

"To go home," I replied, taking Da and Grandpa's hands.

# Chapter 34

We landed with a boom in the middle of the living room as the windows blew out all around us. It was as if I had brought the storm right into the house with us.

"Amelia, what's happening?" Da yelled, as chairs and tables flew around us. And then, with an awful roar, I could hear the house begin to shudder and shake. All this time I had never thought what would happen if I kept using my powers. And now I couldn't stop it.

"Duck!" Grandpa yelled out as a tree branch blew in.

But it was too late. Everything went black.

When I woke up, I wasn't in my house any more. I wasn't sure where I was. For a horrible moment I thought I was still back on Sometimes Island. But I couldn't hear the howling of the wind, or the trees shaking, or the screech of animals. Then Hettie's face loomed over me. I screamed and tried to struggle up from under a blanket.

"It's all right," Da said, "they're here to help us."

In their pyjamas the old ladies looked totally different, not scary at all. In fact, Penny beamed as she fussed over everyone, Pipi chasing at her heels. Only Hettie looked stern. Although the more I looked at her, the more I realized how tired she looked too. She was wearing an old moth-eaten nightgown that hung off her shoulders and her neat white hair wasn't tied up in its usual tight bun. It hung long and limp right to her waist. For the first time I realized how very old she was.

"How long have I been here?" I asked.

"A couple of hours," Da said. His voice wobbled. Pipi barked and licked his hand.

"It's all right now, look! She's going to be OK," Penny said, fussing over my da and pulling a blanket up around his shoulders. "He's not moved from your side. He wouldn't even change out of his wet clothes."

"Grandpa?" I mumbled.

"He's fine. A bit of a bump on the head. But he was making as much sense as usual before he fell asleep," Penny said, pointing to a snoring Grandpa wrapped in a layer of blankets. Pipi trotted over to him and dutifully curled up on his lap.

"It's you we have to worry about," Hettie said, looking down at my flickering hand.

"Here, drink this, it'll help. An old home remedy helps with tummy troubles and all sorts of more magical ailments," Penny said, passing me an enormous cup of something that smelled like cinnamon and spices and, oddly, Marmite.

I took a sip. It tasted worse than the mystery cheese Da had bought on sale in the local shop once. But my hand stopped flickering so madly.

"What's happening?" I asked.

"The power the rock gave you is trying its hardest to fulfil your wish."

I knew when we had crashed into the house that I had lost control of the magic. No matter how hard I tried to stop the disappearing happening, it was determined to take me to one last place. I pulled out the compass; the needle was spinning and spinning like I'd never seen it before.

"But if it succeeds, the island won't be safe, will it?"

Penny nodded. "The storm is only getting worse," she said.

Da had been right when he said I was a proper

255

islander: my home was with him on Dark Muir. It had just taken me a long time to realize that. And now I had, I was going to do everything to protect it.

"How do I stop it?" I asked.

"Come with me," Hettie said as she pushed the door to the attic staircase open.

I picked my way across the attic floor. It was just as cluttered as before. It wasn't long before I tripped up over a pile of magazines and knocked over a lamp shaped like a horse head.

"You best be careful, you don't know what kind of animals you might wake up. Wasn't long ago we had a bear up here," she said, giving me a crooked grin.

I blushed and dug my hands into my pockets.

"Over here, look," she said, wiping away the frost from the window.

I could see out over the snowy cliffs, and beyond the harbour to the dark black sea, and just for a moment, I thought I saw something. Then lightning flashed and the room filled with shadows.

"Can you see it?" Hettie asked.

I pressed my nose up against the cold glass. The moon was out and so were the stars, and even through the storm, they were brighter then I had ever seen them, so bright that I had to squint. But this time I was certain. Out in the ocean, just beyond the harbour, poking out of the sea, was the tip of Serpent's Tooth Rock.

Lightning forked through the sky and the rumble of thunder that followed shook the whole house. My hand burned and my fingers flickered. I could feel the magic tugging insistently at me again, desperately trying to take me to my mum. But it wasn't what I wanted. Not any more.

"I want to give my wish back," I said.

Hettie's golden eyes glinted in the dark and there was a ghost of a smile on her lips.

"Then we need to hurry," she told me.

# chapter 35

It wasn't long before Hettie, Penny, Da and me were all squeezed into Da's old jeep.

"So what now?" Da asked.

"We get Amelia to the harbour and hope I can remember what to do next to help her take back the wish," Hettie said, getting the seatbelt tangled up in her nightgown.

"You don't remember?" I said.

"It's been a long time since I did this last," Hettie replied, blushing.

"But even if you could remember, there's no way we can get to the rock. The harbour has been hit worst by the storm. I don't think any of the boats will have survived," Da said.

But then I had a brainwave.

"*The Bonny!*" I said. "It's moored on Seal Beach."

"That's a sheltered cove, there's a good chance it's still in one piece," Penny said.

"So you're telling me we're going to drive through a snowstorm to get to Amelia's pirate ship so you can hopefully remember how to take back a wish granted by an ancient rock?" Da asked.

"Yup," Hettie said, nodding enthusiastically.

It was the kind of impossible plan that Tom would have come up with. And I realized if it was going to work I would need his help most of all.

"We need to make a stop; I need to get Tom," I said.

Da sighed heavily and slammed his foot on to the accelerator. The jeep lurched forward and we sped off into the snow.

It was already getting dark by the time we reached Tom's grandma's farm. The storm was getting fiercer and fiercer and I could hear the ponies stamping in their pens. I knew Tom would be in there trying to calm them down. I jumped out of the jeep and sprinted over.

"Tom!" I yelled over the paddock fence.

Tom's head appeared from behind the hatch as the fence posts were ripped out from around us.

"Amelia! What are you doing here? Follow me!" Tom yelled, and I ran with him to the barn.

It took both of us to pull the door shut against the wind. Inside I could hear my heart thundering as the wind shuddered and shook the barn around us. The ponies stamped and panted.

"What are you doing here, Amelia?" Tom said, smoothing one of the ponies' manes.

"The rock's back so this is my only chance to take back the wish."

"Are you sure?" Tom said, his eyes growing wider.

"I'm sure," I nodded. "But I need your help."

Tom grinned. "I thought you'd never ask."

The sky was filled with storm clouds. You couldn't even see the stars as we pushed *The Bonny* out into the water. The sea was dark and frothy and it rippled as if something was lurking beneath it. I thought of the fairy tale book from Sinclair's shop and the picture of the great sea serpent. I shuddered as I imagined it moving in coils under the water.

"Get in," Da said and he pulled me and Tom into the boat. I held out my hand for Hettie but she just shook her head.

"Aren't you coming with us?" I asked.

"Not enough room in the boat. Besides, you and the boy will know what to do."

"Good luck!" Penny said, giving the boat a final push into the waves.

"Hold on, this is going to be a bumpy ride," Da shouted, pulling the oars through the choppy waves.

As we rowed further and further out, the boat got pulled from side to side. I had never felt so seasick and Tom clung to the sides with both hands, his eyes shut. But I couldn't close my eyes because just out of the water I could see the sharp tip of Serpent's Tooth Rock. In the dark of the night it glistened.

"Are you sure this is going to work?" I asked Tom.

"I know it will," Tom said.

"This is as close as I can get without running us into the rock beneath," Da said, pulling the oars back into the boat.

We swayed and rocked back and forth, the hull of the boat bumping up against something dark in the water. But even though I could see the tip of Serpent's Tooth Rock, I knew we were too far away.

"I can't reach it," I said. "I'll have to swim for it."

"Don't even think about getting into the water, not with the currents here in this weather," Da told me, spray from the waves falling all around us.

"That's it, then. We came out here for nothing. The

storm will swallow up the rock and the island!" I said, collapsing into the hull of the boat.

"Amelia, you're not going to give up just like that, are you?" Tom cried out.

"I don't know what to do. And Hettie and Penny are not here to help."

"But I am. And I know how to bring the rock back. That day in the girls' loos, when I tried to give you the book, I was going to tell you about the standing stones and how touching them helps bring the rock back up out of the sea."

"That must be what Grandpa was trying to do when he went missing!" I said. "But only the tip of the rock is back, not the whole thing!"

"Not yet," Tom winked. "Because you need this next part..."

Tom leaned his long body over the edge of the boat, his arms reaching towards the rock. He wiggled his fingertips until they just brushed the edge of the rock. Then he squeezed his eyes shut and whispered the words from the final page in the book.

*"Latha a choinduibh."*

The boat wobbled, then, with a huge creak, it was thrown back. Me, Da and Tom hung on to each other. And with a huge roar, Serpent's Tooth Rock rose from the water.

"It's your turn now," Tom said to me.

"I'm scared – what if it doesn't work?" I said.

"Do you trust me?" Tom asked.

I nodded.

"OK then, it's time – time to take back the wish," Tom said.

I looked out at the rock. It seemed so far away and the storm was growing fiercer and forcing us further and further from it. I tried to reach out for the rock but I could see the dark, churning sea below.

"You have to do it now!" Da said, "I can't hold the boat here much longer."

But no matter how hard I tried to be as brave as the women in the book of adventurers, this time I couldn't stop being afraid.

"I promise, whatever happens, I'm not letting go," Da said as he put his arms tight around my waist.

"And neither will I," Tom said as he grabbed hold of me too. "You can do this, Amelia!"

I could feel Da and Tom's grip and I knew that no matter what, they wouldn't let go. And maybe I wasn't as brave as Amelia Earhart, or as daring as Lady Hester, but right then I didn't need to be, because I wasn't alone. I took a deep breath and leaned over the edge of the boat.

My fingertips grazed the rock and, with a final

effort, I pressed my palm flat against the rock.

"I take my wish back," I whispered. "I take it all back!" But the rock didn't move.

"You have to say it like you mean it," Tom said.

I screwed my eyes tight shut and said in my bravest voice, "I don't want to disappear any more."

But I could feel the pull of the magic. In the middle of the storm my powers felt overwhelming. My hand was red hot and the compass shook in my pocket. I knew it wanted to take me to Mum, to finally fulfil my wish. And a part of me still wanted that too. All the things of Mum's I had found when I disappeared popped up in my mind. The binoculars, the fossil, the pirate flag, the sea-worn glass and finally her letter. I thought all of them had been about finding Mum. About making sense of what had happened before she left. But the more I thought about them, the more I realized that all the clues I had found were all about Da. It was Da's boat we had watched for with Mum's binoculars. It was Da who had given me Mum's fossil when I was sad. It was Da who had helped me sail *The Bonny* when Mum couldn't. It was Da who had found me in Puffin Cave and cleaned sea glass with me when I'd been upset, and it had been Da who had hidden the letter, thinking he was protecting me. Maybe in a way the rock had been trying to show me where I belonged all along: with Da, who loved me no matter what.

I reached out with both hands and yelled as loud as I could:

"I don't want you to take me to Mum any more!"

As my voice rang out into the wind and rain, I realized for the first time that I meant it.

For a moment, nothing happened, but then Serpent's Tooth Rock began to shake.

"It's working!" cried Tom.

The rock started to shudder up from the sea, growing taller and taller until it loomed higher than I had ever seen it. Then, with a crack of thunder, the sky filled with light.

"What's happening?" Tom asked as green, yellow and purple lights filled the sky in great waves. The sky shimmered, the lights grew brighter and brighter as they arched above us.

"It's the Northern Lights," Da said, "but I've never seen them so clearly."

"Does that mean it worked?" Tom asked.

I looked down at my hands. My fingers had stopped flickering and I couldn't hear the roar of thunder any more. I pulled the compass from my pocket. The needle wavered for a moment and then stopped. It pointed to where I belonged: past the sea and the beach, past the hill and the cove, and onwards, towards the little white house that lay under the North Star.

"It's done," I said, before sinking back into the boat and into Da's waiting arms.

The last of the storm clouds faded away until there were only bright, brilliant lights dancing above us.

# Chapter 36

After the storm, the whole island woke up to smashed windows, broken roofs and trees torn from the ground. We even got more time off school because the storm had been so bad that it spread to Stony Island too. Bridlebaine Academy had been completely flooded. But it wasn't just the school or the island that had suffered from the storm, it was our house. Not only were all the windows broken, but the tree outside had smashed into my room. It was only Hettie and Penny who had saved us from having to sleep in all the mess.

"You're to keep staying with us until you get your house fixed up," Hettie had said, and after everything that had happened, me and Da had been too tired to argue.

It took us a little while to settle in to living at Hettie and Penny's. Grandpa at first insisted that he would rather "live in the cold and the damp and risk dying from pneumonia". But it didn't take long for him to strike up a friendship with Penny. Every morning they would do the crossword and gossip about the people in the village. Now that Grandpa had a friend, he didn't seem to get so frustrated when he forgot things and he had even stopped doing his "Magical Ways to Pop My Clogs" lists.

It turned out that we all quite liked living at Hettie and Penny's. Da spent the evenings cooking with Penny. Every week they came up with new and slightly unconventional recipes, like Stargazy pie with lobster instead of white fish, fried bread jam sandwiches and vegetarian haggis. It was all delicious! And it wasn't just the food that I liked. Hettie turned out to be one of the kindest people I knew. She spent ages helping me with my schoolwork and listened to me talk about horrible Blair Watson and how anxious she made me.

"Don't you worry, sooner or later that girl will get a taste of her own medicine," Hettie muttered, her yellow eyes flashing dangerously.

Even Pipi seemed to prefer living at Hettie and Penny's. Mostly because every morning after I fed her she would find Hettie and pull her sad face.

"Oh, look at Pipi's poor little face. You must have forgotten to feed her again?" Hettie said.

"Don't trust her for a minute," I said for the thousandth time.

"Oh, but the poor thing looks half-starved," Hettie said as Pipi rolled over on to her back to let Hettie rub her belly. "Have your nasty owners let you go hungry again?"

"Hungry? She's better fed than me or Amelia! In fact, I think she's getting a bit round," Da retorted.

"Shh, don't listen to those bad people. You're beautiful," Hettie said, pulling a biscuit from the packet on the kitchen table and offering it to Pipi. But before she knew it, Pipi had jumped up, grabbed the whole packet and rushed out of the door, leaving a shocked Hettie standing there still with the biscuit in her hand.

"We tried to tell you," Da said.

"It's not their fault; Pipi is a master of deception," I said. "Remember the time she ate Grandma's Christmas turkey?"

"And we had to pretend it was us so Mum wouldn't get upset," Da said.

"And then she found half a turkey leg under the armchair," I finished, laughing.

Penny smiled and nudged Hettie.

"What?" I asked.

271

"Oh, nothing, it's just good to see you two getting on," Hettie said as Pipi wobbled back in, thumping her tail on the kitchen floor as she licked the rest of the biscuit crumbs from her hairy face.

After the repairs were finished we moved back into our house. That's when I finally felt ready to reply to Mum's letter. But even though I had so much to tell her, I couldn't seem to find the right words. It was weird. I had spent the whole year telling Mum all my secrets, but now I could talk to her for real, everything felt different. I had all these mixed-up feelings.

"How does the first night back in your own bed feel?" Da asked as he settled himself into his old position at the bottom of my bed. Then he noticed that I was clutching Mum's letter. "You're going to read the ink off those pages," he said, smiling sadly.

He was almost right; I had read Mum's letter about a million times, but there were still so many things I didn't understand. There were so many questions I still had. And I had been keeping them locked up in my little brain box for so long that now they all came tumbling out at once.

"Was it my fault Mum left? Was it because I wasn't good at schoolwork and I wasn't brave and I wasn't—"

"Amelia, no," Da interrupted. "None of this is your fault, do you understand?"

"Then why did she leave?" I said, my voice small and cracked.

"Your mum wasn't happy living here. She always wanted to go off on adventures. And when your grandpa came to live here, she knew I'd never leave. Our fights just got worse and in the end she felt she had to make a move on her own."

"But why didn't she take me with her?"

Da sighed.

"Because she knew this was where you belonged. This island is my home and Grandpa's and yours."

But this still didn't feel like a proper answer. I used to believe Mum was on far-flung adventures, but now I knew that wasn't true. Now every time I tried to write something to her I just thought of her in her Edinburgh flat, living a life without me. It made me feel all kinds of mixed-up emotions that I didn't know how to explain.

"She just left us, she just disappeared," I said, as tears began to fall furiously down my face.

"I know," Da said, putting a big arm around me. "And I'm not going to tell you that was OK. I think even your mum knows that. But you know it's all right to feel angry and sad and confused with someone and still love them too."

"Is that how you feel about Mum?" I asked.

"Sometimes," Da said.

I wondered if Da was secretly disappointed he had to stay on the island and look after me.

"Da," I said looking up at him in the pale moonlight. "Didn't you ever want to go on adventures with Mum?"

Da shook his head.

"Amelia, you are my greatest adventure," and he looked at me with enough love to light a million stars.

I couldn't help myself, I started sniffing and gulping and then the tears came all over again.

"And I promise you whenever you want, whenever you're ready, I will help you write a letter to your mum," Da said, as he wrapped his arms tight around me and pulled me into one of his almighty bear hugs.

There were lots more things I wanted to ask. And lots more things I knew Da wanted to tell me. But for once it didn't matter that we didn't have the right words, because all the important things had been said.

# Chapter 37

It had been four months since we rowed out in *The Bonny* and I touched Serpent's Tooth Rock. Nobody could forget the storm or the appearance of the Northern Lights that had followed it. Even those who hadn't known what had happened told stories about it. But nobody at school apart from Tom knew the truth. How we had raised the rock and taken back my wish. Ever since that day my secret power had gone and I wasn't sorry. Even standing in the great hall ready to read in the end-of-term assembly, I didn't for one moment wish that I could disappear.

"Could everyone who is doing a reading please line up behind the stage," Miss Rutherford called, waving her arms around like a conductor.

"Amelia Hester McLeod," Miss Rutherford called.

I winced at hearing my full name.

"What possible reason do you have to be out of your line? Do you want to delay the entire assembly?"

"No, miss, I just need to go to the bathroom," I lied.

"If we can teach puppies to control their bladders I will never understand why we can't teach children. Very well, Miss McLeod, but make it quick." Miss Rutherford nodded.

I darted off, ignoring Miss Archibald motioning at me from the stage. I could see Tom waving madly at me from the back of the hall.

"Is everyone here yet?" I asked him.

"Your da and grandpa are in the back row. But I haven't seen the others," Tom said.

My stomach churned. Even though I'd spent weeks writing my essay with Da, and rehearsing it over breakfast, I suddenly didn't feel as confident as I had been in Hettie and Penny's kitchen.

"Amelia, are you sure you want to do this? Because if not I have a plan to get you out of it. We just need tin foil, rubber gloves and a Bunsen burner..." Tom started.

But before I could hear any more of Tom's plan, I was being called back to the stage. On my way over I saw Blair Watson flipping her recorder menacingly. I remembered that she was part of the musical demonstration that concluded the end-of-year assembly, but we both knew she didn't know how to play. She had spent most of our music lessons copying Beth's fingering and just pretending to blow into the recorder. She took her seat at the front of the assembly along with the rest of the musical section that included all the ponytail gang. That day their hair was done in complicated French braids and tied with magenta ribbons.

"You're a dead woman walking," Blair said, and she tried to trip me up with her recorder as I passed her on my way to the stage.

I got back into line just as everyone settled down in the great hall. The lights dimmed and Miss Rutherford's bangles jangled up and down her arm as she stepped forward to introduce the assembly. Then Miss Iris stepped forward to talk about her class's art project and show off the weird sculptures they had made. Followed by Mr Norris, who talked about the books and plays we had read this year. Then Chloe read out her essay, which was brilliant and somehow made *A Midsummer Night's Dream* sound like it wasn't the most boring play in the world. After everyone clapped, Miss Archibald appeared and started talking about our journal project. Backstage, I felt like I needed to pee and throw up both at once. I had never been so nervous. There were so many people out there and I knew Blair and the ponytail gang would be waiting for something horrible to happen to me. I even wished I had stuck around to hear more of Tom's mad tinfoil and rubber glove plan. But before I knew it, Miss Archibald had called my name.

"Good luck," Chloe said and gave my shoulder a friendly squeeze as she came off the stage and went to sit down in the empty seat next to Blair. I looked out at the sea of ribbons and felt even sicker.

As I stepped out on to the stage, Miss Archibald's blue exercise book felt like it weighed as much as a Galapagos giant tortoise. I could barely open it as I took my place at the lectern stand.

"My Year of Disappearing," I read out nervously into the microphone.

There was a little gasp of excitement and then the hall settled into quiet. Everyone stared up expectantly. Except for Blair, who whipped out her phone.

I tried to ignore her, but when I looked down at the page again all the letters seemed to swim about. I felt a shiver of panic as I looked out over the sea of expectant faces. I opened my mouth again. I knew what I wanted to say, but I could already see the words getting tangled up on the page.

"Oh my God, this is too good; either she's going to

disappear in front of the whole school or she's going to wet her pants," Blair stage-whispered loud enough so I could hear.

But then the doors of the hall burst open. Everyone turned around to see a whirl of handbags and umbrellas and long tartan skirts getting tangled up in the double doors.

"So sorry we're late," Hettie said, striding down the gangway. "We were unavoidably detained by a small dog trying to eat an entire wardrobe full of old shoes."

"Did we miss it?" Penny asked.

"Amelia was just beginning and there are a couple of spare chairs at the back," Mr McNair said.

"Oh no, I won't be able to see anything from all the way back there!" Hettie said.

Both Hettie and Penny barged their way to the front, pushing children out of the way so they could get as close to the stage as possible. After a brief, noisy musical chairs, they ended up sitting right behind Blair.

"Where were we?" Miss Archibald said, taking the stand again and trying to quiet everyone down.

"Amelia was just freezing up…" Blair sniggered.

Then I saw a quick flash of something slip out of Hettie's handbag. There was a loud snip and then Blair jumped up screaming. The whole assembly let out a scandalized "Ooooh!" But it took a moment

279

for me to realize what had happened: Hettie had cut Blair's ponytail clean off.

"WHAT HAVE YOU DONE?" Blair roared, hopping from one foot to the other.

I could hear the collective creak of everyone leaning in to watch.

"I was just trying to trim my nails and my hand must have slipped," Hettie said coolly.

"She did it on purpose!" Blair screamed.

"Oh no, Hettie's just very clumsy. It's what happens at our age, isn't it, dear?" Penny said, doing her very best to keep a straight face.

Then something very odd happened. Blair burst into tears.

"I'm sure it will grow out!" Hettie called as Blair sprinted howling from the hall.

"Settle down, settle down!" Mr McNair said, standing up, but it took a full five minutes and Miss Rutherford bellowing at everyone before the hall fell into quiet again.

"Are you ready to start again?" Miss Archibald asked

I looked down at my essay. The words bulged and jiggled and even without Blair there, I wasn't sure I could get through it.

"If you wouldn't mind, I think we would like to make just one more interruption," Hettie said and

Miss Archibald stepped aside as she clambered up on to the stage with Penny.

"How about we read this together," Penny whispered in my ear as she put her finger on the word I needed next.

I looked out over the crowd again. But this time I spotted Grandpa and Tom giving double thumbs up and right beside them was Da, beaming and full of pride. I took a deep breath and in my loudest, bravest voice, I said:

"My name is Amelia Hester McLeod and this is the year I learned about wishes."

Then Hettie burst into life talking about the myth of Serpent's Tooth Rock. She was every bit as scary on stage as she had been when she tried to warn me that first time in my kitchen. And then Penny joined in, and before I knew it we were all telling the story together. Everyone laughed when Penny got overexcited pretending to be the storm and nearly fell off the stage and there was a large gasp when I told the part about me disappearing in the middle of the night. It didn't seem to matter that some bits of my essay got left out and other bits got added in.

In fact, by the time we got to the night of the big storm, it felt like the whole room was waiting. Waiting for what came next. Hettie and Penny looked at me and nodded. I looked down at my essay. It had taken me ages to write the end; I had crossed it out and rewritten it with Da so many times that I knew it off by heart. But even so, I tucked the essay back into my blue book. Because it didn't feel like it was just my story any more.

"Tom!" I called, squinting over the lights.

Tom sank down in the row at the back. But even squashed down in his seat, he was still heads and shoulders taller than everyone else.

"Tom!" me, Hettie and Penny chorused.

Reluctantly Tom stumbled his way to the front and climbed up on the stage.

"The thing is, it was Tom who saved the day," I carried on. "He was the one who knew the magic words to say that would bring the Serpent's Tooth Rock back."

Tom blushed so hard that even the tips of his ears went bright red.

"Amelia, you know I'm not good at talking in front of people. I don't want to get word vomit and mess up the end of your story," he whispered.

"You trust me?" I asked.

Tom nodded and I handed him the microphone.

"Well it wasn't all me. It's just I knew what to do. But first we had to get to the Serpent's Tooth Rock and all we had was an old rowing boat."

282

Once Tom began, he couldn't stop. But for the first time, it didn't matter, because the whole assembly was listening to every word. Even when Tom got all squeaky and breathless telling the bit when the boat almost capsized, nobody laughed. And when it got to the end, Tom finally took a breather so I could describe the appearance of the Northern Lights in the sky as the storm faded away. How they had shone above us, brighter than we had ever seen them.

When it was over, I could feel how quiet the hall had grown. I could hear the ticking of the clock and Grandpa sniffing into a hanky. I could even hear my heart thudding in my chest. I wondered for an awful moment whether Blair's horrible friends were going to point and laugh or if I was going to get a detention for doing the assembly all wrong. But then Da stood up and started clapping and everyone else joined in. Tom grinned and grabbed my hand and we took a ridiculous panto-style bow.

After the readings we were all led off the little stage to the room at the back. I couldn't believe how many people wanted to come over to congratulate me. It felt like the whole school had something to say about my speech, even Chloe.

"I just wanted to say well done, Amelia. And I'm

sorry I've been bit rubbish to you this year," she said, awkwardly looking down at the floor

"I might have been bit rubbish to you in the past," I said, thinking of all the mean things I had said to her after my mum left.

"Maybe we can try and be friends again?" she asked, pulling at her hair nervously.

For the first time I noticed she wasn't wearing her purple ribbon. In fact, when I looked around, no one was any more. It was like seeing Blair cry had broken some awful spell.

After I'd said goodbye to Chloe and Tom, I made my way out to the reception where Da was waiting.

"Amelia, I just wanted to tell you that…" Da started as he rubbed his beard trying to find the right words, "that was really not bad, not bad at all." I could see his eyes were shining with proud tears.

Then Miss Archibald appeared, clapping her hands together.

"Bravo, that was wonderful, Amelia. A bit more creative than I had expected, I must admit. But it was a really fantastic story. I'm so proud of you," she said before she peered at me over her glasses.

"It was just a story though, wasn't it? In the corridor after your fight with Blair I thought I saw…" Miss Archibald trailed off, knitting her brows together. "But I couldn't have, could I?" she finished as she shook her head.

I opened my eyes as wide as I could to give my most innocent "I don't know what you're talking about" face.

Miss Archibald raised one of her thin rainbow eyebrows. But then she smiled.

"You have a very talented storyteller, Mr McLeod," Miss Archibald said.

Da looked down at me. His face was beaming.

"Yes I do," he said with a wink.

"I very much look forward to reading what you write next year," Miss Archibald said before she headed off to the great hall again.

Da put his arm around my shoulder as we walked down the corridor and into the sunshine outside.

# chapter 38

On the morning of my twelfth birthday, I was standing in the harbour wearing mismatched wellies and holding a lobster. This is exactly how birthdays should start.

It was so early that the stars were still out, but I didn't mind. It was as if the sky had put up fairy lights just for me. Me and Da clambered into the newly repaired boat. We hadn't been on the water together since the night of the storm. Da nervously rubbed his freshly shaved face.

"I miss my da the yeti," I said, grinning.

"I wanted to remember what my chin looked like," Da said, grinning back.

I suspected the lack of beard had less to do with

Da's chin and more to do with Miss Archibald, who had been making more and more excuses to talk to Da about my "progress" at school.

"Come on, Pip," I said with a whistle.

Pipi eyed the boat suspiciously before leaping and landing inside with a thud. Pipi had got a lot bigger over the summer. It probably had to do with all our visits to Hettie and Penny's. There always seemed to be tea and cake and, for some strange reason, bacon. Pipi stuck her cold nose under my armpit and we set off.

The light came up fast as we sailed out of the harbour. The days were getting brighter and brighter. But Serpent's Tooth Rock loomed larger than ever. When the boat rocked to a standstill in its shadow, Da rubbed his big furrowed brow.

"Are you sure you want to do this?" he asked.

I nodded my head. It had been nearly four months since I last disappeared, but I still had one thing left to do.

"Can we do presents first?" Da said.

I grinned and nodded and Da pulled out three of the most beautifully wrapped presents I had ever seen. When he saw my shocked face, he flushed pink.

"Hettie and Penny helped with all this," he said, pointing to the bows and ribbons and sparkly paper. Pipi helped me unwrap the first by tearing through the paper with her teeth. I had to put the bow on her head to stop her. Her big eyes rolled up to stare at it, as she thumped her tail with approval.

"It looks good on you, Pip," Da said as he laughed.

I let a book slip from the torn wrapping paper. It was the old fairy tale book from the bookshop. *The Myths of Dark Muir* gleamed in gold letters.

"Tom helped me find all the rest of the book and we got Mr Sinclair from the bookshop to glue it back together," Da said. I flicked through it, remembering the dark scary forests and the brightly lit sea caves and the strange stone circle. All the places on the island I had disappeared to over the year.

"Do you like it?" Da asked.

I nodded. I didn't know what to say. This was the first time I had ever liked a book without facts.

"Maybe you can read me some of the stories. As long as none of them come true," he winked as he passed me another present. I unwrapped it to reveal a yellow book with gold-edged pages and a red ribbon bookmark.

"It's a journal. I thought it was about time for a new one," Da said.

I smoothed my hand over the soft cover. It was much nicer than my old exercise book and this time I was looking forward to writing in it. In fact, I was looking forward to writing all sorts of stories in it. Miss Archibald had been so impressed by my story I told in the assembly that she signed me up for her special creative writing group. And even though I still liked lists and facts and things that didn't have confusing full stops, it was quite fun writing stories when you had help. Plus, Tom had already promised to do all the pictures.

Then he passed me a familiar small red box. Inside was Mum's compass. But the glass had been fixed. The gold case no longer had a dent in it and on the back, engraved under Mum's initials, were my own. Da picked it up by the new gold chain and slipped it over my neck.

"Just in case you ever get lost again," Da said.

But I knew I didn't need any help finding home. Not any more.

When I looked up again, Da nervously passed me a thick envelope. I recognized Mum's scratchy handwriting right away and my heart leaped. Earlier that summer, just as Da had promised, he had helped me finally find the right words to put in a letter to Mum. And I had waited for one in return ever since.

I pulled off the paper and into my hand slipped a brand-new copy of *The Little Book of Lady Adventurers*.

Inside Mum had written:

For the adventurer I am most proud of.

"I told your mum how your last book had got ruined and how you missed her reading you bedtime stories. So she's going to call you tonight," Da said.

I pressed the book into my chest, feeling all the love Mum had sent with it. I couldn't have asked for a better birthday present.

"So are you ready?" Da asked. In all the excitement of opening presents I'd almost forgotten what we'd came out to do.

Da helped me over the side of the boat and I reached out to touch the rock; I had one last thing to say to it. Because even though I hadn't got what I wished for, the rock had, in its own way, brought us all back together.

"Thank you," I whispered.

This time the rock didn't move; it didn't even twitch. It felt cold and still. But I knew it was just sleeping.

When Da pulled me back into the boat I could tell he wanted to ask what I had said, but he didn't. Instead he put a big arm around me. We sat in the boat listening to the sound of the waves slapping against the hull. A gentle breeze blew over the water as the stars faded away into the bright morning sky.

"This is my favourite part of the day," he said. "Just before everything happens."

"Mine too," I replied.

The island flickered in the distance as the sun climbed behind it. From the boat I could see our house, the last glow of the North Star shining over it. Grandpa would be sleeping in his chair downstairs, a forgotten cup of tea lying next to him. Later he and I would play chess the only way we knew how, with lots of yelling and throwing of things. And then I would go over to Tom's and we would ride the ponies late into the evening, before Hettie and Penny threw a not-so-surprising surprise party, including ridiculous home-made party hats and the biggest, bluest cake you have ever seen. Afterwards, Mum would telephone to read me the stories of Amelia Earhart and Lady Hester and then we would talk late into the night. But this was going to be my favourite part of my birthday. Sitting in the boat with Pipi and Da, watching the sun come up over the island. This strange place I called home, where magic and myth could take you on incredible adventures.

*Discover more about the incredible, intrepid women adventurers who inspired Amelia…*

# AMELIA EARHART

*July 24th 1897 – July 2nd 1937*

A spirit of adventure burned bright in **Amelia Earhart** from childhood – she was a tomboy who loved to be outside climbing trees and riding her sled fast downhill.

She would grow up to become the first woman to fly solo across the Atlantic, a huge and dangerous undertaking. On May 20th 1932 she took off from the Canadian island of Newfoundland and landed safely in Ireland nearly fifteen hours later, despite facing strong northerly winds, icy conditions and mechanical problems. That same journey would take four-and-a-half hours in a plane today.

Amelia was a passionate believer in equality and independence for women and encouraged many to fulfil their dreams of becoming pilots and soaring into the sky.

In 1937 Amelia Earhart and her navigator Fred Noonan were on one of the last legs of an epic around-the-world-flight, when their plane vanished over the Pacific Ocean. They have never been found and this disappearance has become one of history's great unsolved mysteries.

# LADY HESTER STANHOPE

*12th March 1776 – 23rd June 1839*

A true rule breaker, **Lady Hester Stanhope** disguised herself as a middle-aged man and travelled incognito across the Middle East, at a time when women were expected to sit quietly and meekly at home.

She was born into the aristocracy and could easily have spent her life cosseted by comfort and luxury. Instead, she chased adventures – these were often fraught with danger, such as the time she survived a terrible storm at sea and a shipwreck in which she lost all her possessions.

She had a particular interest in archaeological digs and unearthed some wonderful treasures. Lady Hester went where she wanted and did as she pleased – she was bold and fearless and was always in search of new, exciting horizons.

# ALEXANDRA DAVID-NEEL

*24th October 1868 – 8th September 1969*

Originally a French/Belgian opera singer, **Alexandra David-Neel** converted to Buddhism and travelled to the Forbidden City of Lhasa, Tibet – which at the time was completely shut off from foreigners. She disguised herself as a beggar and a monk and hid a pistol, a compass and a purse of money under her rags, in case she was captured and held to ransom. There, she reported witnessing levitation and the practice called *tummo* or inner fire meditation, where the body raises its temperature to combat the extreme cold felt at altitude in the Himalayan mountains.

When Alexandra David-Neel was one hundred years old, she applied to renew her passport, clearly planning on further adventures. Sadly she died aged one hundred and one before she could embark on another trip, but left behind a legacy of a life dedicated to exploring.

# HELEN THAYER

*Born 12th November 1937*

**Helen** was born in New Zealand and has spent her life to date travelling across some of the most challenging, hostile and remote corners of the earth.

In 1988, she became the first woman to travel solo (though with her dog Charlie for company!) to the magnetic North Pole. From snow and sub-zero temperatures to exposure to scorching sun: she has also walked across the Sahara Desert and 1,600 miles across the Mongolian Gobi Desert. And from dry land to river rapids: she has kayaked over 2,000 miles in the Amazon rainforest.

Helen has been named "One of the Great Explorers of the Twentieth Century" by *National Geographic*.

# KATE JACKSON

*Born February 14th 1972*

**Kate's** specialist subject is … snakes! And the more venomous the better, though she says she feels no fear while she is working. She first encountered a snake at the age of five, which led to her fascination with them. After studying snakes at university, she travelled to Central Africa, specifically the Republic of Congo, where she battled through an infection that began in a tiny scratch on her leg, and caused extreme dizziness and a high fever as she made her way alone through the jungle. She recovered and went on to discover a brand-new species of snake – the Radford's House Snake.

She has had a few close calls with her slippery subjects – she was allowing a small snake to slither through her fingers when she suddenly realized it was a highly venomous baby forest cobra and needed to be put down very, very gently!

# BERYL MARKHAM

*26th October 1902 – 3rd August 1986*

**Beryl** was a famous pilot, adventurer, racehorse trainer and author, best known for her solo flight across the Atlantic Ocean from east to west. No woman at the time had flown non-stop from Europe to North America, though a few had set off and died in the attempt.

On the 4th September 1936, Beryl took off from Abingdon in England on the trip of her lifetime. 20 hours into the flight, ice collected on her plane's fuel tank vents, causing Beryl to crash land on Cape Breton Island, Nova Scotia, Canada. But she survived the landing and achieved her mission to reach North America – she would be celebrated as a true pioneer of air travel.

# ANNE BONNY

*Unknown, possibly 1697 – unknown, possibly 1782*

One of the most famous female pirates of all time, **Anne Bonny** sailed the seas of the Caribbean in the eighteenth century, capturing many trade vessels and stealing their treasures.

Records state she had red hair and a fiery temper – she embarked on a lawless life on the waves alongside John "Calico Jack" Rackham, captain of the pirate sloop *Revenge*, feared by all. She was captured but there is no record of her execution: did she escape prison and return to her life as a pirate? We'll never know for sure…

# JUNKO TABEI

*22rd September 1939 – 20th October 2016*

**Junko** was the first woman to reach the summit of Mount Everest, the tallest mountain in the world, and the first woman to ascend all Seven Summits by climbing the highest peaks on every single continent on earth. These are:

Asia: Everest; South America: Aconcagua; North America: Denali; Africa: Kilimanjaro; Europe: Elbrus; Oceania: Carstensz Pyramid.

She let nothing stand in the way between her and the very top of the mountains: she survived a major avalanche when climbing Everest, which buried her camp under a deep, suffocating blanket of snow. She survived and twelve days later reached the peak of this dangerous mountain, the first woman to stand on top of the world. It was an astonishing feat of determination, bravery and resilience.

# IDA PFEIFFER

*14th October 1797 – 27th October 1858*

**Ida** travelled all across the globe, at a time when most women were not permitted to dream big. She was born in Vienna but visited Brazil, Chile, England, America, Australia to name just a few countries – writing about the places, people, customs, landscapes, flora and fauna she saw, so that others may experience her adventures from their own homes.

She had a strong desire to see the world from childhood and made this dream a reality: forging her own path across the world, on her own terms.

# ADA BLACKJACK

*Unknown month, 1898 – May 29, 1983*

**Ada Blackjack Johnson** was born in Alaska, and in 1921 she joined a five-man expedition to Wrangel Island, north of Siberia, in an attempt by Canada to claim the island as its territory.

Conditions were harsh and inhospitable, with sub-zero temperatures and ferocious winds. After rations ran out, three of Ada's fellow explorers attempted to cross the seven hundred mile frozen Chukchi Sea to Siberia for help and food. None of them were ever seen again. Meanwhile, Ada had been looking after the fourth man back at the camp, who was severely ill with scurvy and soon died, leaving Ada alone and at the mercy of the extreme elements. She had just the expedition's cat, Vic, for company.

Ada was eventually rescued from her terrifying arctic adventure – with newspapers calling her a "female Robinson Crusoe" after the famous fictional castaway.

# LAURA DEKKER

*Born 20th September 1995*

**Laura** is the youngest person to ever sail solo around the world: an astonishing achievement at any age, but she was just sixteen when she set sail on her voyage, which lasted for one year and five months.

She has a Dutch father and a German mother and grew up in New Zealand and the Netherlands. Brave and single-minded, she has sailed the waters of some of the most dangerous places on earth, such as the Cape of Good Hope, coping with dead calm (no wind for the sails) and howling gales and rough currents.

But even a brave adventurer such as Laura couldn't escape going to school! She continued her studies throughout her time at sea by taking online courses to keep her caught up with her friends.

# ACKNOWLEDGEMENTS:

There were a lot of times I thought this book would never happen. It is entirely down to the support of those mentioned below that it did. My heartfelt thanks goes to my family and friends for supporting, encouraging and generally putting up with me while I wrote this. To Mum, Dad and Ryan for nudging me on, to Rose for reading the very first page and Kelly for buying me the odd drink when it was much needed. Thanks also to my agent Hellie who believed in me and this story from the start. And who read and gave notes on so many wobbly drafts. To my editor Lauren, who with one inspired change ended up shaping this book into something far better (books really are made in the editing). Thank you to all the fantastic team at Scholastic and Janklow and Nesbit UK for their hard work. To the Hawthornden Castle Fellowship, who allowed me to be their writer in residence and pretend to be a Scottish Queen. And finally thank you to all those who buy, borrow and review this book.

© Kelly Boyland

Amber Lee Dodd teaches creative writing, has a blue belt in kickboxing and briefly lived in a Scottish castle. Her dream is to go on an adventure to the Arctic, or to ride across the Arabian Desert, like the lady adventurers in *Lightning Chase Me Home*. But she mostly spends her time by the sea dressed in 1940s clothes, coming up with stories.

Her plays have been performed at the Minerva Theatre, New Theatre Royal and the Edinburgh Fringe. Her short stories have been published around the world and broadcast on BBC Radio 4. Her first book, *We Are Giants*, was nominated for ten awards, winning the Calderdale Book of the Year and shortlisting for the Branford Boase Award.

Follow her on Twitter @amberleedodd
www.amberleedodd.com